MOM AND DEAD

ONE

The view from Andrew Broom's offices on the twelfth floor of the Hoosier Towers in Wyler, Indiana, was an illustration in perspective. Straight lines vectored toward an infinitely distant point where they would meet. No mountains or even significant hills arrested the eye. Andrew Broom, a native of the Midwest, found the view conducive to thought or, as at the moment, a welcome relief from a boring client.

"So what do you think, Mr. Broom?" Jerome Blatz sat back, having said his piece. Susannah had tried to take Jerome's cap when he came in, but he would have felt naked without it. Above the bill was an American flag and the legend, "These colors don't run." Only a native of Wyler would know that Jerome could buy and sell half the town and have money to spare.

"If the price is right and you want to sell the land, I don't see how you can go wrong, Jerome."

"But that's the question. Do I want to sell?"

That had been the question for half an hour. If

Jerome sold, he would face the problem of investing the profit. His inclination, as always, would be to invest in real estate. And the land he was being asked to sell was exactly the kind of investment he would be looking for.

"Not that I would pay what I'm being offered."

"How much would you pay?"

Jerome turned his head and looked slyly at Andrew out of the corner of his eye. "I thought we agreed we could talk without my saying what the offer is."

"No, Jerome, *we* did not. You stipulated that, and only after you got comfortable in that chair." Andrew stood. "You don't want to keep paying me for my time when you don't trust me enough to say exactly what we're talking about."

"Now take it easy, Mr. Broom. Just sit down. I'll tell you."

"Good." Andrew remained on his feet.

Jerome tipped back his head to squint up at his lawyer. "First I'll tell you that the offer is twice what I believe the land is worth."

Andrew sat down, no longer tempted by the view.

Susannah brought in coffee, poured, and, from behind Jerome, tapped her watch. But Andrew had ceased to care that the appointment was running over the allotted time. His attention had been unexpectedly engaged.

"Start over, Jerome. Tell me all about it."

The land in question lay along the Tippecanoe River west of town, just forty acres Jerome had used as pasture until he decided to sell off his herd. The kids were grown and gone, there wasn't enough profit from selling milk to offset the expense and time, and forty more acres of soybeans made sense. A man representing the potential buyer had driven into Jerome's place two days ago, having checked out the ownership of the land.

"What's his name?"

"He was with Mr. McGough."

McGough! Why hadn't Jerome said so earlier? Frank McGough was Andrew Broom's rival and had been since they were kids. Instinctively they were on opposite sides of any question. Well, all but one. Neither Andrew nor Frank wanted anything to come of the attraction Gerald Rowan, Andrew's nephew and partner, felt for Frank's daughter Julie, and vice versa. In everything else, they were implacable foes and if Frank McGough had an interest in Jerome's river acres, it was Andrew's fate to oppose the sale.

"I'm glad you didn't just jump at the offer, Jerome."

"No, I didn't. But I won't pretend I don't find it attractive. The fact is, Frank McGough seems to be representing some damned fool who either doesn't know the value of land or doesn't care. If there were any other available river property, I would sell mine and replace it with another hundred acres."

"Have you checked that out?"

"I did."

"And there's nothing else available?"

"Not on the market. But then mine's not on the market. They just drove in and five minutes later flat out made an offer. Andrew, they could do the same to anyone else."

"Then why did they come to you?"

"I *could* say I'm lucky, but you know me."

It was Jerome's affectation that he was buffeted by the winds of ill fortune, lived from hand to mouth, and was lucky to have a roof over his head. It was superstition. To crow about what he had acquired would tempt the gods to take it from him.

"Did you check on that?"

"On what?"

"If any other owners have received offers."

Jerome sat forward. The keys clipped to his belt rat-

3

tled against the chair as he moved. "I didn't turn him down, Andrew. I said, give me some time."

"Maybe he decided to cover his bets. Maybe he's buying up all the land he can get."

Jerome was excited now. His expression was that of a man who was being unfairly treated. "I'll ask around, Andrew."

"You mean you're going to announce to Wyler that someone from Chicago is offering to buy land for twice its value?"

"I'm not going to announce anything. I'll just see if anyone else lets on."

"To you? Why should they? They'd be as cagey as you are."

Jerome sat down, took off his cap, banged it on his knee, and then set it far back on his head. "Damn it, Andrew, I have to find out."

"That's why you came to me, Jerome. Leave it in my hands."

Relief gave way to a flicker of wariness, then returned to settle on Jerome's weathered face.

"Good. You're my lawyer, you represent my interests."

"I could do no less, Jerome."

Jerome took his used cup out and handed it to Susannah. When he saw who was waiting for an appointment, he turned and looked suspiciously at Andrew. Bink Philips stared over his magazine at Jerome.

"You been arrested or something?" Bink asked. "Is that it, Jerome? You in trouble with the police?"

"How long you been out here?" Jerome asked.

"All the while Andrew's been arranging bail for you."

There was no natural end to such rustic humor and Bink was enjoying himself so much it was all Susannah could do to tug him past the infuriated Jerome into the office. Andrew accompanied Jerome to the door.

"What the hell's he doing here?" Jerome asked in a fierce whisper.

"He's been arrested."

"C'mon."

"We'll put up the bail and he'll be on the streets again today."

Jerome wore a betrayed look as he silently departed. He had trusted Andrew and it had come to this.

"Andrew," Bink said, still chuckling, when Andrew settled behind his desk. "I want you to do the paper work on a land sale."

TWO

Bonnie was working the horseshoe-shaped counter reserved for truckers and things were slow. She put her weight on one sneakered foot, rested her hip against the counter, and dragged thoughtfully on a filter-tip menthol cigarette. She could remember ads promising her that smoking this brand was like taking throat medicine. A trucker whose mouth scarcely moved was telling her of traffic a hundred miles east he'd driven through.

"You ever thought of ventriloquism?"

"What?"

"You know, you get a dummy, hold it on your knee and make it talk."

"Is that a proposition?"

"I mean it."

"So do I."

He had a day's growth of beard, the squinty eyes of a driver on the alert for trouble, an oversize nose. No prize, but what the hell. Bonnie was getting dangerously close to fifty. Not that she thought the guy meant anything. Talking dirty to waitresses was part of the job description. The legend on his tee shirt was Truckers Do It in Low Gear. His baseball cap had a Pirates emblem. He was waiting to see if she did mean something. She let her lids droop and dragged again on her cigarette while she imagined asking him to stick around until she got off. They could go to a motel, she wouldn't take him to her place, and have a time. Who knows what she might have done if Jack hadn't sailed in from the truckstop garage?

"Joe," he hollered, not even looking at her, going on to the cashier. She poured his coffee and put it on the counter opposite the trucker. Did anyone besides Jack call coffee joe anymore? Joe, java, all those funny names for it. Now even truckers asked for decaf, as if they were afraid they might not fall asleep behind the wheel.

Having bought a pack of cigarillos, Jack slid onto a stool, breaking into a smile when his eyes met hers. God he was good-looking. Blond curly hair he wore long, the bluest eyes, and built like a weight lifter. They called him Mr. Goodwench, but he was the best mechanic in the garage, and many a trucker had limped along for miles just to get to the Indy Truckstop where Jack could look over his rig and see what the hell was wrong. For a second or two, she held his full attention, but then he looked across at the driver.

"How long you been here?"

The driver looked at Bonnie. "Ten minutes?" It felt like more, because of his boring account of the traffic, but ten was probably right.

"Any other drivers been here?"

Bonnie resented it that Jack should ask the driver. Whose station was this, for God's sake? The driver suggested that Jack ask Bonnie.

"Bonnie?" The corners of Jack's mouth went down

7

and he turned his head slightly. "I thought you'd only been here ten minutes."

The driver tried to let it go, not sure whether Jack was kidding. Bonnie wasn't sure he was kidding either, and she liked it. Just when Jack got her mad at him he turned around and put her on a pedestal. Imagine, resenting a trucker calling her by her name when it was pinned to the front of her uniform, engraved blue letters on white plastic. Bonnie might have intervened, but she didn't. She stepped out of the station, leaving the two men confronting one another from opposite sides of the horseshoe. She looked around to see if any of the other girls had noticed, but they were busy blurs, speeding around on crepe soles or sneakers, wearing expressions of happy harassment. Phyllis, carrot red hair caught in a green snood, glanced at Bonnie but kept on going through the swinging door into the kitchen. Phyllis had as much as said that Bonnie was robbing the cradle with Jack and laughed her bucktoothed laugh when Bonnie told her it was Jack who came on to her. That was the truth but she felt like she was lying when she said it. If Jack was going to punch out a driver for calling her Bonnie she didn't want Phyllis to miss it.

The driver picked up his check and sat sidesaddle on his stool, waiting to see what Jack intended to do. If they got into it outside, no one would know what it was about.

A gleaming semi, all chrome and white, its body outlined with lights, went slowly past the windows, its musical horn playing Popeye's theme song. The driver broke into a grin and Jack did too and when they went out the door together they might have been old buddies rather than two men who had been on the verge of fighting over her.

"Shoot," Bonnie said and got back into the horseshoe to collect the cups.

THREE

The glitzy rig slid past the pumps, still playing that tune. Beside Jack, the driver began to sing. "I love to go swimmin', with bowlegged wimmin." Jack punched him on the arm and headed back to the garage. A six-wheeler, all dents, rust, and mud, came around the big rig and drove right into an empty bay in the garage. Jack waited until the driver was out and gone. It was part of the routine that they never talked, never even looked at one another. Jack clambered up into the cab, closed the door, and sat, breathing deeply, wishing it was two hours from now.

No other mechanic would wonder what he was doing sitting behind the wheel, eyes closed. He cultivated the reputation of having a mystical connection with anything on wheels. All he had to do was sit in a rig and he would understand exactly what it was the driver was trying to tell him was wrong. With his eyes still closed, he felt the panel of the door, then drew out a screwdriver.

It was never the same truck twice, maybe it was never even the same driver, maybe the driver wasn't even in on it, though he'd have to be a damned fool not to wonder at the instructions he was given. What didn't change was where the stuff was.

The screws were rusty as if they hadn't been off since leaving the factory. Once that would have bothered Jack, but he knew it didn't mean a thing. When he replaced the panel, he would spray the screwheads with gunk and they'd look the same way. He fed the screws into his shirt pocket as he removed them, just the top ones, until he could pull back the panel and see the bag inside.

He removed it, put it inside his jacket, then took an envelope from his jacket pocket and slipped it behind the panel. After buttoning up the panel, he sprayed the screwheads back to their rusty condition. Two minutes at most. He closed his eyes again, pressing the package against his side with his arm, keeping his mind a blank.

But he never could. Sometimes he imagined himself confiscating the package and going free lance. He had a rough idea what he could make on the street with it. The only trouble with that was he might do it once and then he wouldn't be doing much of anything ever again. Still, it was fun to imagine himself really rolling in money. He'd open his own place . . .

Sometimes, like tonight, he was bothered by images of school yards, kids playing and yelling and having fun the way they did when he was a kid. There was no junk in Wyler in those days, kids didn't even understand the lyrics of the songs that celebrated it. Jack had heard the claim that it was available back then, he just hadn't known about it, but that was like saying things were no worse than they'd ever been, there was just more publicity nowadays.

Jack Parry didn't believe that for a minute. The country was going to hell even faster than Grover Layton, minister at Christ's Own Temple said in the rip-roaring sermons Jack loved to listen to on Thursday nights. He took Thursdays and Sundays off, fouling up his weekend just so he could be there when Layton preached. The tide of evil sweeping across the nation was visible to anyone who had eyes to see—pornography, child abuse, divorce, sex all the time, television. It helped to know that things were bad no matter what he did. Why shouldn't he make a few bucks out of the debacle, particularly since he tithed at the temple? It was Grover Layton's conviction that we were well into the Book of Revelations, with the end coming when we least expect it, the Lord God reserving special vengeance for the town of Wyler, Indiana, whose sins rose up like a stench in the nostrils of the Almighty. It made Jack feel better about his divorce too, and about Ellen raising Tommy all by herself.

FOUR

Ellen's friends all told her how smart she'd been to get rid of Jack. "Take him for all he's got," Louise had said, as if Jack had money in the bank or something. What he had—what they had—it became clear, was a mortgage on the house, taken out at an interest rate that made her lawyer shake his head.

"We'll refinance that as soon as we can, Mrs. Parry."

"I'll get the house?"

"It would serve him right to let him take it, but he'd just sell it for the equity."

"How much is it worth?"

Mr. Hawkins hummed as he figured. "Not much. You wouldn't clear two thousand dollars."

What she got was the right to pay the mortgage, Tommy, and a loneliness that was welcome for a week or two and then began to make her feel as if she had been drummed out of the human race. She divorced Jack—"got rid of the sonofabitch," as Louise put it — but she was the one who felt rejected and abandoned.

"Free again." Louise said it with a jealous smile. Louise had been threatening to get out of her marriage long before Jack's playing around broke up Ellen's, but she was still toughing it out with Willis, while telling Ellen she had done the right thing, and suggesting that now Ellen could have one hell of a time if she wanted to.

Maybe she herself had imagined that after the divorce things would be as they had been during those two or three years after high school, years of carefree fun as they seemed now, though there had been anxiety wondering when someone nice would want to marry her. When Jack Parry asked her out she figured it would be a night spent fighting to keep him off her and that would be that, but she was so flattered about going out with such a good-looking guy that she decided to take care of trouble when and if it arose. If it even looked like trouble when it did. But Jack had been a gentleman, opening doors, getting her settled in the car before he went around and got behind the wheel, constantly interrupting himself as he told her about his prospects at the truckstop to say, "But tell me about you."

She had never felt more dull and uninteresting, but she had wits enough to tell him she'd much rather listen to him. When he took her home, he walked her up to the door and, after an awkward moment, put out his hand. As they shook, she leaned forward and kissed him on the cheek, then went inside.

That impulsive kiss on the cheek did it, if Jack could be believed. He said he drove aimlessly for an hour afterward, telling himself I have just gone out with the girl I want to marry. And he did marry her and it wasn't until their honeymoon that they made love. It seemed a good omen, it seemed to say that he respected her. He saw her as his wife, mother of his children, not like . . . But at that time she hadn't known about the other girls, quickies, as he called them, they didn't mean a thing.

"They mean a thing to me," she said, not believing he expected her to go along with it. They made love maybe once a month and it was nice, she never said otherwise, but that wasn't near enough for Jack.

"Have I ever said no?"

"I don't want you to be like that."

Like the quickies, apparently, whatever that meant. Did he think she didn't enjoy it? He couldn't explain it.

Well, she did try to live with it, she really had no choice, and it was their secret as far as she could tell. He didn't make a spectacle of himself. Whoever his girls were they seemed to exist in another world, totally unrelated to their neighborhood in Wyler, Bel Air, a suburb where ranch houses sat on lots from which all the trees had been removed before construction began. The scraggly little trees, lovingly tended, that now stood on the green lawns would need half a century to look real. People made up for it with evergreens and shrubs. Ellen was so proud of the house when they moved in. The neighbors were a notch or so above them but Jack made a hit with the men, largely because he could talk cars better than anyone, and Ellen got along with the women even though many of them had a year or two of college and sometimes talked of the books they were reading. Ellen had her hands full with Tommy.

Knowing Jack had other girls affected their life together; she couldn't help wondering where he had been and when, and she began to fear he would bring home some awful disease. She talked to Louise about it, very indirectly, as an abstract problem.

"I'd castrate Willis if he ever did that," she said vehemently. Willis was six and a half feet tall, bald as an egg, and homely in a nice sort of way. Louise was a head shorter than Ellen and had a bad habit of telling how rotten it was going to bed with Willis.

Fear of disease made Ellen cold to Jack; she began to

put him off, but he didn't complain, he seemed happy about it. They had Tommy, he didn't want any more kids, and by now Ellen had figured out that he thought sex was dirty and he didn't want it at home because home was different. So that part of her marriage was all but over. By the time Tommy was seven, she and Jack were down to maybe two or three times a year. Ellen felt that they had entered into an official pact, with her giving her blessing to the quickies.

Not that he talked about it. The whole point, it seemed, was to keep that sort of thing away from her. Would things have just gone on like that if Willis Long hadn't seen Jack with a girl and told Louise? Louise came right on over, got settled at the kitchen table with a cup of coffee, and announced that she knew all about Jack.

"What do you mean?"

Louise lowered her eyelids and looked askance at Ellen. "Oh come on."

It had been up to her, Ellen saw that later. If she had just played dumb, not even Louise would have pressed it, but like a nerd she burst into tears and then she was telling Louise the whole story.

"The sonofabitch."

She tried to explain to Louise that it really wasn't that bad, Jack was good to her and Tommy, but even as she said it she knew how funny it sounded. Louise's advice was to lock him out of the house, but there was no way Ellen was going to do that. She loved Jack, at least she thought she did, she didn't want a divorce.

"You'd be *free*, Ellen."

"Free."

Louise's eyes sparked at the prospect of liberation from Willis, that "goddam house," the kids. "He'd get the kids, I'll tell you that. I'd visit and all, but he could have them day to day. See how he'd like that."

If she left Jack, Ellen would want Tommy. What would she be without her son? In the end Louise convinced Willis to say something to Jack and then the fat was in the fire. He was furious to think that anyone knew about their intimate lives, let alone Louise and Willis Long. Willis never changed the oil in his car, his back fender was rusting; such negligence disgusted Jack. As for Louise, from the beginning they didn't get along.

"Too gushy," he said.

"What a movie star," Louise said, and it sounded like a criticism.

Ellen tried to explain to Jack but he wouldn't even listen he was so mad and then he moved out and she seemed caught up in a process she could no longer control. Louise arranged for the meeting with Mr. Hawkins, Ellen kept waiting for someone or something to stop it, but no one did. She called Jack at work and they talked, mostly about Tommy and the moles in the backyard, but she sensed that he would never forgive her for talking to Louise about their life together. She would never forgive herself.

So she ended up free, with a mortgaged house and an eight-year-old son. She got a job in the school cafeteria, and at night after Tommy was in bed she sat staring at the TV as if she had just landed from outer space and was trying to get the hang of this new planet.

Tommy was Jack all over again, except that with him it was science not cars. He put together some apparatus Ellen couldn't begin to understand and won the first prize at the science fair. He had decided he wanted to be a doctor and all his teachers told Ellen that she had a very very bright son. For his birthday he asked for a plastic skeleton of the kind medical students use and Jack chipped in and they bought it for him so that whenever Ellen went into his room she was met by a full-size skeleton dangling from the ceiling on its invisible wire. The bones seemed never to be still, and their faint clacking gave her the shivers.

Tommy's shelves were filled with jars and bottles, specimens, and he had his chemistry lab set up in a corner. And then one day when she made his bed, she noticed the skull on the shelf. Unlike the skull on the medical supply house skeleton it was not chalk white. She looked away when she first noticed it but then couldn't stop herself from staring at it. The holes where the eyes should be seemed to watch her and the yellowish teeth grinned relentlessly. But it was the neat hole through the forehead that drew her to the shelf.

How real the skull seemed. She put out her hand tentatively and touched the hole in the front of the skull. Immediately she drew back her hand. Where on earth had Tommy gotten such a thing? Of course it couldn't be real.

Only it was.

"I found it," Tommy said.

"Where!"

That had been a mistake; she had frightened him and he clammed up. "Take it if you want it."

"I don't want it! I want it out of here."

He nodded, not looking at her, and Ellen felt that she had failed some test. The worst part of trying to raise him alone was that she made all the mistakes. Jack wasn't there to make any so of course Tommy must wish he was with his perfect father who wouldn't ask dumb questions about all the things Tommy insisted on keeping in his room. She told him he could keep the skull.

"What's that smell?" Louise asked, sniffing, flaring her nostrils, her plucked brows lifted.

Tommy was in his room doing chemistry.

"Chemistry!" Louise said. "How old is he?"

"He's smart."

Louise resented that and who could blame her, given the trouble her kids had in school.

"He'll burn the house down."

Louise insisted on looking in on Tommy and screamed when she saw the skeleton dangling from the ceiling. Even Ellen laughed.

"Where in the name of God did you get that?"

"It's not real, Louise."

Louise, holding her nose, went to see what Tommy was cooking up. And then she noticed the skull.

FIVE

Gerald Rowan had come to Wyler fresh from law school and the editorship of the review, turning down two gold-plated offers in Chicago to join instead his uncle's firm in Indiana. Mrs. Commers in placement had laughed when he told her.

"You're not serious."

"Yes."

"But why?"

"He's my uncle."

"If he loves you he won't want you to throw away your career before it's begun. I assure you, once you've gone to—where is it?"

"Wyler. Wyler, Indiana."

She closed her eyes and waited for the pain to pass. "You would be burying yourself there for life. I don't care what your record here has been, none of it would matter. It's now or never."

"I've decided." There seemed no point in telling her of the golf courses, one designed by Arnold Palmer. She was not at all impressed by Uncle Andrew's argument that he would know more variety of legal practice in one year in Wyler than in a lifetime in Chicago.

"This is the age of the legal specialist. It's no different than medicine. There is no need for the general practitioner."

"I am grateful for all you've done."

Mrs. Commers looked reproachfully at him. He had been the apple of her eye; she had taken him aside and arranged interviews for him long before posting the visitation hours of the representatives of premier firms. When the offers had come, she had cried out with pleasure, hugging herself as she did so. Now he had come to give her what she had to regard as disastrous news. For a moment, Gerald himself doubted the wisdom of his decision. But then he remembered dinner at the country club with Uncle Andrew and the beautiful girl to whom Andrew refused to introduce him.

"Is she married?"

"No."

"So what's wrong?"

"She's a McGough."

The beauty had looked his way and Gerald felt electricity pass between them. She felt it too. Her mouth opened slightly before she turned away. The man with her glared at Gerald.

"Frank McGough," Andrew said through locked teeth.

Two championship golf courses, a girl he had not even met, and a legal prospect he would not have imagined could tempt him had brought him to the decision that so disappointed Mrs. Commers.

Gerald never regretted it. The golf courses were twin dreams, their fairways seldom crowded, beautifully tended. He met Julie McGough and their relationship, despite the disapproval of her father and Andrew, prospered. Her golf game was formidable and it was the struggle, not always unsuccessful, to beat Gerald that drew her closer to him. The term love match took on new meaning for Gerald. Two falls out of three. If he had been less of a competitor he would have deliberately played below his game and taken the conquering heroine to bed. As it was, competition quelled their ardor. From time to time, they played as partners and it was during these more serene rounds that they agreed they were meant for one another.

"Never," Andrew said. "As in never."

"My father says he would see me dead first," Julie reported.

"We could elope."

She shook her head. Her heart was set on an elaborate wedding. It was a problem. So was the mysterious stranger seeking to purchase land along the Tippecanoe River.

"There's no pattern to it," Andrew said. He was poring over a map of the area. "This is Blatz's piece. Here is Bink's."

The two pieces of land were separated by a strip of land on which a road gave public access to the river.

"Are those the only pieces he's after?"

"I don't know."

He looked at Gerald. He would not willingly pronounce the name Frank McGough.

"I'll see what I can find out."

Andrew gave a slight nod, as a sinner deceives himself that he is not assenting to what he does. The simile was no accident. That night Gerald and Julie went to a revival and listened to the impassioned sermon of the Reverend Grover Layton. The tabernacle seemed a place where no one they knew would be. The listeners rocked and sweated in their seats as Layton with obvious relish painted a picture of corruption, degradation, and wickedness. Gerald's hand stole toward Julie's. Her palm was moist in his and their grip tightened as the rhetorical tide rose. They jumped to their feet when others did and their hugging and kissing blended with the general excitement. The idea had come to Gerald while watching an old wartime movie in which a couple much in love went to a train station where they could cling to one another to the general indifference of those really arriving or departing.

Afterward they drove out to the Indy Truckstop where they had huge greasy burgers served in a plastic basket with chunklike french fries. The section reserved for truckers filled and emptied, other travelers came and went; the waitress wore her red hair in a green snood and chewed gum as if her life depended on it.

"Jerome Blatz was in the other day," Gerald said.

"What did the preacher mean by eschatology?"

"He never used the word."

"He did. When he quoted from the Apocalypse."

"Revelations."

Julie smiled. "We call it the Apocalypse." Her every expression was more beautiful than the last. Beneath the table her knees pressed firmly against his.

"Read my apocalypse."

She stuck out her tongue. Julie was a Catholic for whom the Bible was a closed book. She had hesitated about attending a Protestant service. It's why she couldn't elope. They'd have to bring the priest along. She laughed when he suggested it.

"You don't know Father Foley."

"I'm looking forward to meeting him."

She looked sad, a tragic figure. He knew that in part she enjoyed the star-crossed nature of their love. Would she have been attracted to him if there were no impediment to their union?

"What about Jerome Blatz?"

"A client of your father's is trying to buy some land from him."

"I don't know anything about it."

"Same thing with Bink Philips."

The waitress came and took away their plastic baskets after refilling their coffee mugs.

"So?"

"There could be others. I'd like to know."

"Why?"

"Because my uncle won't just pick up the phone and ask your father."

"I'll see what I can find out."

"My place or yours?"

"Ha."

"I love you."

"Words."

"I had action in mind."

"Not until we're married."

"Talk to your parents."

She shook her head. "Not yet."

He could have waited a million years for her, and he almost said it. On the other hand, any delay was a knife in his heart. But how could he reproach Julie when he did not dare to tell Uncle Andrew he intended to marry the daughter of his arch and lifelong foe?

SIX

Jack never stayed the night, which was okay with Bonnie, but she didn't like the way he bounded out of bed as soon as it was over and started dressing. She complained about it.

"I feel like a whore."

He laughed. He was a different man now, having got what he wanted. When she was younger she would have been really hurt.

"I got to get going."

"Got a date?"

He frowned. "Thanks."

"Oh you're welcome."

"What's wrong?"

"Nothing."

He was fully dressed now and obviously impatient to go. "Okay?"

Asking permission to go? Well, he might just have taken off and ignored her. She couldn't be mad at him.

"Get out of here," she said. "Just leave the money on the dresser."

She rolled toward the wall, tugging the blanket over her shoulder. She heard the door close and, before sleep claimed her, the sound of his car starting outside. Twenty minutes later she was awake again, lying on her back, staring at the ceiling, thinking of Jack and the truckstop and then the floodgates opened and the whole melancholy story of her life seemed to play itself out like a sad movie. Jack was typical of her life, something nice but she only had a small claim on it.

It really wouldn't have mattered if he had stayed, because in the morning he would be gone, the night soon forgotten. Nothing lasted. That was the one lesson she had really learned. Maybe that's why she kept making the same stupid mistakes over and over again. Good things didn't last but neither did bad. Life was slipping away. Even lying on her back in bed, her body felt heavy. She was losing her shape, or gaining another, depending on your point of view. It was the Indian blood in her, at least that was her excuse, one sixty-fourth some tribe or other, her mother had been vague. Not that it meant anything to her. Her brother Clark's wife had become a fanatic about it, sitting out there in their mobile home, writing letters to the paper, writing a newsletter that went to every shirttail relative she could find out about. Bonnie never read it. Phillipa convinced Clark that the reason nothing went his way was because the white man had cheated him out of his native heritage.

"You want land, Clark? You want to be a farmer?"

"This land was ours before the white man came."

His authority for this was Phillipa, who did research on local history at the historical museum and proved to her own and Clark's satisfaction that his forebears had been cheated out of their homeland.

"Well, if they were, the crooks were your other fore-bears. And there's more of them in you than Indian. We're one sixty-fourth, Clark. Maybe one sixty-fourth."

"That's the only part that matters."

He believed that now. To hell with him. It was a nitwit dream that some day a Brinks truck would pull up in front of his mobile home and drop off zillions of dollars in compensation for the injustice done to a fraction of Clark's family tree.

Bonnie said, "How many Hoosiers do you think got some Indian blood in them?

"Leave her be, Flip," Clark said. "To hell with her. I've got more important things to do than try to convince a goddam dumb truckstop waitress that it matters what blood runs in her veins."

Bonnie didn't want anyone at the truckstop to know she had even the little bit Indian in her that she maybe had. Was she ashamed of it? It just wasn't something she was proud of. She didn't think Clark was proud of it either. He got mad as hell when she kidded him that there was black blood in their veins too. He threw a beer bottle at her and damned near hit her and Phillipa had to shield her so she could get safely out of the mobile home and to her car.

"Don't joke like that, Bonnie."

Phillipa was not yet thirty, the third wife Clark had had, twenty years younger than he was, and she was telling Bonnie what to do?

"I'll remember that."

"Bonnie, this is serious. It's the one thing he takes seriously. He's quit drinking."

"Maybe he should go back to it."

"Go to hell."

So both Clark and Phillipa were mad at her, big deal, what had they ever done for her?

SEVEN

Andrew called Susannah from the car to tell her he was going out to look at the land Jerome Blatz and Bink Philips had come to him about. Wyler had spread east and south but here to the west the farmers' love of their land kept things much as they had been when Andrew was a kid and a day spent fishing or swimming in the Tippecanoe seemed the purpose of life. Andrew's return to Wyler after five years in an Indianapolis firm had been meant to reclaim his life. He had excelled in law school, been more than ensconced in the firm, his future was an ascending line. Success was assured. So was boredom. He missed the full range of the law, but to stay in the firm was to specialize. A general practice in the city was unlikely to be as profitable. He decided that if he were to make that switch, he would make it in Wyler where prosperity and variety could be combined.

And where he could resume his competition with Frank McGough.

Their rivalry had begun in grade school, ripened in

27

high school when the esteem of girls had been added to the competition in sports and grades. Doing well in Indianapolis, Andrew was aware that Frank was doing at least equally well in Wyler, on his way to becoming the premier lawyer. Coming back to Wyler had been a declaration of war.

Ever since, battles had been lost and won but the major issue was left in doubt. Neither man could settle for a divided and shared triumph. For Andrew to hear that he and Frank were the two best lawyers in a hundred-mile radius was gall and wormwood. Each man sought a primacy that eluded him.

Andrew turned off the county road onto the public access trail and pulled his car into the shade where he switched off the motor and sat listening to the country sounds crescendo to his ear—a whir of insects, the warble and caw and twitter of birds, a far-off dog tirelessly barking. High above, the trail of a jet fattened in the blue sky. He opened the door and got out, angry at the fleeting thought that this road would dull his shoes with dust. As a boy he had gone barefoot to the river, his step quickening at the thought of settling down to the prospect of hours of fishing.

Gerald had verified from Julie McGough that Frank was representing an out-of-town client interested in riparian rights on the Tippecanoe River. To get the stretch he wanted, he was going to have to buy four parcels of land and deal with cagey locals who had never before thought of their riverside land as valuable. Jerome Blatz's piece of land had twenty feet of riverbank from which it wedged wider as it moved toward the county road. Bink's piece would add thirty yards.

"Who are the other two?"

"One. Wendell Jensen has two pieces they want."

"They?"

"Frank McGough and whoever."

When he was a kid, Andrew had never thought of the riverbank as owned by anyone, it seemed a common possession. The farmers who owned the land along the Tippecanoe apparently felt the same way, as long as kids kept out of their fields. In hunting season, that land along the river wasn't even posted, strengthening the illusion that these were public lands.

Long before he reached the riverbank, Andrew had removed his coat and tie. Now he sat in a patch of shade created by a clump of sumac and looked out over the slowly moving water. If he closed his eyes he was sure he would hear the shouts of swimming boys, companions long since grown up and, for the most part, gone from Wyler. But he did not close his eyes. He was not here on a sentimental visit. Someone was trying to buy up this land and he wanted to know why.

To the north, at New Carlisle, a Japanese steel giant had built a huge plant on what had been two family farms and the region had prospered. At night, flying home to Wyler, Andrew had looked down at the vast illumined complex. It might have been a city unto itself.

There were other possibilities too that would be good news for the town. He tried to take comfort from the thought but his unease would not go away. Was he acting like a kid, miffed because Frank was involved in the deal? Would he begrudge the town good fortune because he had nothing to do with it? Not a pleasant thought but, he admitted, it represented at least part of the explanation of his uneasiness.

He sat there for ten minutes trying to think of the bad things the land purchase might mean, but the best he could come up with was that it threatened to alter a place that was still exactly the way it had been when he was a kid.

When he got up, he went back to his car through the little woods between Bink Philips's corn and the river. A kid was suddenly there, as if he had been conjured from Andrew's memories. He was rattled by the appearance of an adult and looked at Andrew in a way that suggested he was up to no good. Andrew looked around.

"You alone?"

"Yes."

"I'm Andrew Broom. What's your name?"

"Tommy."

The kid was holding a plastic sack behind him, as if to conceal it, and Andrew found himself siding with the kid and resenting his own intrusion. It seemed a violation of a place meant only for the young. He checked himself before telling Tommy that he had played here when he was about Tommy's age. What bores kids more than that kind of remark?

"Just Tommy?"

"Parry."

Andrew nodded and started toward the access road, leaving the woods to Tommy. What was in the plastic sack? It was none of his business but he amused himself on the way to his car imagining that it was a turtle or some such treasure a boy would want to take home.

EIGHT

Louise said she really didn't care what Willis thought, and she didn't. It was hard enough to get the dumbo to forget the television long enough to hear a word she said, but trying to remember the last time she'd had a conversation with her husband was like trying to remember the last time being in bed with him was anything but a bore. Louise had read somewhere that the mark of the irrational animal is its undeviating pattern of behavior, each repetition of a deed the exact replica of all the preceding. As a lover Willis was an irrational animal. In everything but passion.

Their whole life was just the same thing over and over again. He woke her in the morning, clattering around in the kitchen, always making the coffee too strong no matter what she said, banging around before he left so she almost never got back to sleep. Once the kids were in school and she had the day to herself life was tolerable, at least most of the time, but she couldn't help feeling jealous of Ellen Parry, rid of Jack.

Ellen had played it all wrong, letting her Romeo of a husband get off scot free, sticking her with house payments and the kid and a lousy job at the school cafeteria. Of course, Ellen should have had the wit to hang onto a husband like Jack. There is only one way to keep a man from roving. Louise was convinced that even if she had been dealt Ellen's hand she could have made it pay.

"You should thank God for Willis," Ellen would say, sounding as if she really meant it.

"Oh, he's a real dreamboat."

"He's true to you."

Louise laughed, not because it wasn't true, but because anything else was unthinkable. Willis's awkward height made him seem silly and watching him get settled in his lounge chair before the television every night, tilting back, raising his legs, sighting in on the screen, ready for several mindless hours, Louise could not imagine any woman in her right mind finding Willis attractive. The man was so dull he couldn't possibly provide her with a legitimate excuse for a divorce.

Is that what she wanted? What she wanted was something more and different from what she had. Ellen envied her and she envied Ellen. Not the debts, not a kid Tommy's age, not the job in the cafeteria, but the freedom. There was nothing to stop Ellen from moving to California tomorrow if she wanted to. Or anywhere else. She could go out nights, meet people, go up to Chicago where she wouldn't run into people she knew, have a good time. A good time. Louise left it conveniently vague in her mind. Her idea of heaven was Hawaii and she was as likely to get there as she was to get to heaven.

What she really envied Ellen was little Tommy, a real Huckleberry Finn of a boy, the son she would have loved to have. And good in school besides. In high school Louise had spent two weeks in chemistry before

getting permission to transfer out and her notion of
brains had become anyone who could figure out chemistry. Yet little Tommy worked away at it in that weird
room of his, full of skeletons and other things a boy's
room ought to be full of. What did a kid that age think
of a father who acted the way Jack Parry did?

"What did you tell him?" she asked Ellen.

"About Jack? That he wouldn't live here anymore."

"What did he say?"

He didn't say anything, if Ellen was telling the truth.
She communicated with her son somehow without
words. At least when he was home. Where did he go
when he went out? Wherever it was he went alone.

But where on earth had he found a human skull?

Ellen didn't know and became angry when Louise
pressed her about it but, for heaven's sake, children
can't be allowed to play with human remains. She made
that point as forcefully as she could to Ellen but all she
got was an outburst of tears and the blubbering request
that she leave her and her son alone.

That had been bad, they usually got along so well,
Ellen listening and nodding as Louise talked. Louise
still had her key to the Parry house, which was more
than Jack did, the idea being that she could look out for
things during the day when Ellen was at work.

"Where would a boy find a human skull?" she asked
Willis, but she might just as well have spoken to the
wall. She turned off the television and stood in front of
it facing her furious husband.

"What the hell are you doing?"

"I am trying to get your attention!"

"You got it."

They glared at one another. Louise inhaled and shut
her eyes. "Tommy Parry has got a skull in his room."

"A what?"

"A human skull."

"Oh come on."

"I saw it myself."

"Listen, you can buy them in stores. It's just the kind of thing kids like. Turn on the set."

She turned it on, wondering if for once in his life Willis was right. What did she know about skulls, real or fake? She had to have another look at it.

The next day she let herself into the Parry home, closed the door behind her, and stood listening to the silence of the house. She had a right to be here, Ellen had given her a key, but she felt sneaky nonetheless. There was the faint smell of Tommy's chemicals and the sound of the radio in the kitchen. Ellen left it on all day, as a house sitter, figuring if anyone broke in and heard the radio they would think someone was home and go. Sure they would.

Louise pushed away from the door and hurried down the hall to Tommy's room. Her breath caught at the sight of the dangling skeleton but she had been prepared for it so it wasn't too bad. She crossed to the shelf. The skull wasn't there.

She put out her hand and touched the spot where she was sure it had been, then turned slowly and looked about the room. Louise blamed herself. Her reaction had alarmed Ellen and she must have told Tommy to get rid of that thing. Or perhaps she had gotten rid of it herself.

Then again, maybe it was just hidden. She looked under the bed and in the closet and through every drawer of the little dresser. How neat and clean his things were, but that was Ellen's doing, of course. Boys weren't neat. Not boys like Tommy. Louise smiled despite herself.

That night, after Willis got settled in front of the television, Louise called the *Wyler Dealer* on the kitchen phone and told them a boy had found a skull.

"Who's calling please?"

"I don't know where he found it, but it was real enough."

"Give me the boy's name."

Louise put down the phone, shutting off the questions. Of course they would need to know who she was and who Tommy was if they were going to print anything. What on earth had she intended to do? Had she imagined readers wondering what kind of a mother would allow her son to play with a human skull? Is that what she had wanted, to humiliate Ellen?

She sat and listened to Willis talking back to the television. What a foolish thing it had been to telephone the *Dealer*. She surprised herself even more when she called Jack about it.

NINE

Fellow classmen at Bloomington had been amused, years ago, when Humphrey Ward told them about the family newspaper back in Wyler. The *Dealer*. The paper had been founded by his grandfather, a printer, and continued by his parents, first his father and then, over some seventeen years by his widowed mother. She had continued to occupy the editorial chair after Humphrey joined the paper. That was the understanding, of course, he would work up from the bottom, but he assumed that the time he'd put in as a high school student and the three summers while he studied journalism counted as his apprenticeship. His mother shook her head.

"Reporter," she said. "That's where your father started."

"But he didn't go to college."

"That's true. He had less to unlearn."

That interview established their relationship at the paper, they were no longer mother and son, owner and heir, but boss and greenhorn reporter. For the first time

Humphrey understood the reputation that Maisie had at the paper, in the town, beyond.

When she took over for her husband it was simply to fill his place. She still thought of herself as the stand-in for her dead spouse, and his name was invoked frequently and with reverence. It was, it occurred to Humphrey, a shield from behind which she could write the acid editorials that set teeth on edge in town and, in political season, elsewhere in the state.

"We are a conservative paper," did service to explain a multitude of decisions and once invoked there was no appeal. Maisie credited herself with an infallible instinct for discerning what fit the paper's policy and what did not.

It was a stern apprenticeship under which Humphrey had risen eventually to occupancy of the editorial chair. Now as the sole owner of the paper he nonetheless portrayed himself as the spokesman of wiser heads. Through him, his parents, or at least his version of them, continued to guide the *Wyler Dealer*. Thus while he listened to the preposterous suggestion of Phillipa and Clark Cooper and prepared his rejection of it, he unconsciously did so in the first person plural.

"I'm afraid that your proposal doesn't fit our present editorial plans."

Phillipa ignored this. "It's a violation of rights. Religious rights."

"Bingo?"

Clark sat immobile in his chair and only his mouth moved when he spoke. "My people need the income from bingo in order to finance our tribal rites."

"Religious rites," Phillipa said emphatically.

Clark Cooper's bingo game, a major attraction at the Bison Bar and Bingo Parlor that the two of them owned, had always been private enterprise so far as

37

Humphrey knew and there was no local opposition to it, unless you counted the rivalry of St. Luke's Wednesday nights.

The Coopers had come to enlist the paper's condemnation of Boyd Carlson's alliance with the legislative cabal seeking to outlaw bingo in the state. It was going pretty far to describe Clark's bingo game as an activity of the breakaway remnant of a verifiable Indian tribe to which he had first declared his allegiance only three years before. The addition of a bogus claim to infringement of freedom of worship doused what little interest Humphrey had in the matter. Besides, the paper had supported Boyd Carlson in four successful campaigns for the state senate as well as his previous terms in the assembly.

"What we'll do is a story on bingo in Wyler and environs. Your activities will figure in it."

It was a good thing he didn't expect the Coopers to be grateful for the free publicity. Of course they might have had some intimation of what the story would be like.

His mother would have liked it. There wasn't an evaluative sentence in it; it was as neutral a portrait as could be painted of the school auditorium at St. Luke's on a Wednesday night, the long paper-covered tables, the constant creak of the folding chairs, the hush when the numbers were read, the impassive expression on the winner's face, the grudging congratulations. Humphrey juxtaposed to this scene a fleeting glimpse of Father Foley in the rectory parlor watching a ball game. Catholics aren't Methodists, of course, and most citizens of Wyler were prepared to make allowances for these legionnaires of Rome. The account of Cooper's commercial game made it clear that a significant number of his customers were to be found on Wednesdays at St. Luke's. Bingo, the article concluded, was the one clearly ecumenical activity in Wyler, Indiana.

Still the question remained: What had gotten into Boyd Carlson?

It was the stated axiom of the *Dealer's* editorial policy that all politicians are either corrupt or on the way to becoming so. Boyd had been in Indianapolis a long time. Of course terms in the assembly or senate were part-time jobs, but the sessions had a way of occupying a member's time in proportion to the length of his or her tenure. Humphrey tilted back in his chair, let his eyes lift slowly above where the Coopers had sat, and engaged the steady gaze of his mother. A photograph. She had vetoed the idea of a painting.

"Warts and all," she had insisted, wanting the wheelchair to which she had been confined to be visible in the picture. The automobile accident that had led to the wheelchair had strengthened her character. It was her total absence of self-pity that had impressed even Humphrey. His mother's expression seemed to endorse the suspicion of Boyd Carlson that had begun to grow in him.

"What do you make of the anti-bingo bill?" Humphrey asked Andrew Broom one night in the bar of the country club.

"Are you coming out for it?"

"Should we?"

"If you want to have the whole of St. Luke's down on you."

"Did you read our story?"

"Of course."

"Over fifty percent of the players are Protestants. At any rate, they are not parishioners."

"Even so."

"Boyd Carlson is a sponsor of the bill."

"Of course he is."

Humphrey looked at Andrew for a moment and then remembered that Boyd was Frank McGough's candidate, not Andrew's. They took their drinks to a table where Andrew began to quiz him about the work of the committee to attract industry to Wyler. The industrial park near the airport was developing nicely, Humphrey thought. Along its wide streets, neat low buildings on grassy plots housed electronics manufacturers, a food wholesaler, a number of businesses with fewer than a hundred employees but a boon to the local economy. Small business was the backbone of the nation, Humphrey had been taught, and he believed it to be true. Wyler was interested in sensible growth, enough to keep the town vital, not so much as to change its nature.

"Do I detect criticism in your voice, Andrew?"

"Not at all. I just wondered if there's anything in the offing."

"Several things."

"Big?"

"Nothing we can't accommodate at the industrial park."

"Anything not at the industrial park?"

Humphrey sipped his drink. Andrew was a poker player and he was showing his hand so the question was what was he concealing. It was of course possible that something was afoot that Humphrey did not know. This was not a welcome thought, and for two reasons. As a member of the committee and as editor of the Wyler paper of record he felt he had a constitutional right to be told of any significant happenings in town. A previous remark of Andrew's seemed to provide the necessary link.

"Are you saying Frank McGough is up to something?"

Andrew lifted his brows, considered his drink, drank. Message received. Of course it was an old rivalry, Andrew Broom and Frank McGough, and one which proved to be beneficial to the community. The two men vied with one another for the role of major benefactor of Wyler and their contest upped the ante of their generosity. Not that Humphrey was neutral between the two men. He did not like Frank McGough. If Frank did not exist, Andrew would continue being a benefactor of the town, whereas Humphrey was sure that without the stimulus of competing with Andrew, Frank McGough would turn a deaf ear to pleas for help.

Andrew having made his point turned the conversation to sport. Bill Gleason's column was carried by the *Dealer* and that alone won Andrew's allegiance, but he also praised the coverage of the local single A team, part of the Reds organization.

Before going into his solitary dinner, Humphrey phoned the office and spoke to the night editor.

"Anything new?"

"At a newspaper? Of course not. Just an anonymous call reporting the finding of a human skull."

Humphrey smiled. It was the kind of story his mother had assigned to him. He decided to put Pascal Pence on it. She was the youngest reporter, but one Humphrey was convinced had the makings of a great one. And he had learned the joys of keeping her half mad at him with the assignments he gave her. Whenever he thought of Pascal he avoided his mother's eyes.

TEN

Bonnie was okay but Jack Parry did not kid himself and he didn't kid her either. She was tail, that's all, amusement, relief, going to bed, nothing more. He didn't say that to her, he didn't have to, Bonnie was no dope. At least he thought she wasn't before she began to tell him about her brother the Indian.

"What tribe?"

"What difference does it make? We've got a sliver of it and that's all. You know what they say about Ivory soap."

"What do they say about Ivory soap?"

He lay on his back beside her, smoking one of her cigarettes, staring at the ceiling. They were resting up for round two and letting her talk was as good a way to pass the time as any.

"Ninety-nine and forty-four one-hundredths pure. You gonna call it impure because of that little bit?"

"Then you're Indian too."

Would her body keep expanding until she was a ton of lard wearing moccasins, her face still pretty? Bonnie was pushing fifty but she looked like a little kid. Her expression. Like she was still expecting something great to happen. Life just couldn't be only what she'd seen so far. That's what her face seemed to say.

"You know what the joke is?"

"I'm waiting."

She rolled toward him, the springs complained, he felt her warmth against him. He imagined the ceiling steepling. Here he was with his squaw in their teepee.

"Chances are Clark isn't even that little bit Indian."

She told him about their mother, hers and Clark's. She had liked a good time as well as the next person. Her husband had been out West working on Hoover Dam for a year before Clark was born.

"Tell him."

"I couldn't prove it to him."

All this interest in learning where you came from left Jack cold. Thoughts of bloodlines and ancestors and family reminded him of what he had done to Tommy and Ellen. His public version was that Ellen had thrown him out, as if it was her fault, not his, but inside he knew he had deserted them, done to his son the same goddam thing his father had done to him. It was like an heirloom passed from father to son to son, on and on, an inability to stick with one woman.

In the army there had been a weak-chinned college boy who sat on his bunk and listened with pop eyes when they got around to talking about what they'd done and to whom on weekend liberty. Ted was his name. Theodore. He explained to them that all this catting around—of course he didn't talk that way, he called it promiscuity—was a mental illness.

"Is that where the mind is located?"

"Yours is," Ted said. "If all these stories are true and not just fantasies. Not that it would matter so far as the explanation goes."

"Why don't you come along and find out?"

Not in a million years, he said, but it was already obvious Ted's curiosity had gotten the better of him. Maybe that was another mental illness. Anyway, they took him down to Tijuana and a few weeks later symptoms of clap showed up and they had fun for quite a while insisting that Ted use the stool set aside for the infected. Ted was so depressed he was put in the base hospital and eventually discharged.

What had that meant? Nothing, except Jack had always remembered Ted's explanation of the way he behaved. Calling it an illness made it sound like something that just happened to him. So he ought to feel innocent. Instead he felt guilty as hell. He shut out the thought of Ellen seeing him lying here beside this fifty-year-old waitress, listening to her babble about her brother the would-be Indian. Did he really prefer this to being home with Ellen?

The question came too late. Ellen had divorced him. He didn't blame her. Not that he had kidded her either. He never pretended to be anything but what he was.

In the bathroom he poured a line and inhaled it through a straw from the truckstop diner. The samples he took from the packages he removed from behind the door panels of trucks had accumulated before he tried the stuff himself. He had to see what the attraction was. Now he knew. He carried some with him in a little Sweet 'n Low sack, also from the truckstop. Once Bonnie had poked her head into the bathroom when he had taken the sack from his pocket. He told her he had diabetes and needed the sugar. Fortunately she didn't notice the sack had contained a sugar substitute.

Sometimes he thought of turning her on to the stuff, but he never did. When he came out of the bathroom, feeling great, it was hard not to want to let her in on it, but he had no illusion about what he had become involved in. Once a week, after the van came through the truckstop, Jack would leave the stuff in a locker at the bus stop, where he'd also find the envelope of money. A different locker every time. How would he know which one? A key was slipped under his door while he was at work. This had been going on for eight months now. He started to skim a couple twenties from the envelope before putting it behind the door panel of the truck. All pretty complicated, it seemed like kid stuff, but these people played for keeps and insulated themselves as much as they could while keeping a tight control. Jack's pay was sent to him at the converted motel where he lived, a money order. What he wanted more than anything in the world was a Porsche and with what he was making he would have one eventually.

Back in bed, he tried to concentrate on what Bonnie was saying. She was talking about what Clark hoped to get out of his Indian connection. His line of defense of his bingo game if the state passed a law against gambling was that bingo was a sacred right of his tribe, something like that.

"It's different with Phillipa. With her it's a crusade."

"She an Indian too?"

Bonnie laughed. "Only by marriage."

The image of Phillipa was a welcome distraction. Jack had seen her when she stopped by the truckstop with Clark to talk with Bonnie.

"That your sister?"

"In-law."

He'd dropped it. No point in getting Bonnie going. The easiest way to get her steamed was to stop and talk with one of the other waitresses. It wasn't just a game of course. Jack was always on the alert for an adventure. That's why he overcame his wariness when Louise Long called. "Sure, I'll meet you."

He assumed it would be about Ellen. Louise was the

neighbor lady who had spurred Ellen on with the divorce. Maybe now she wanted to try to patch things up, get them together again. Deep inside, Jack believed that sooner or later, before it was all over, he and Ellen would be together again. His mental illness aside, she was his wife and nothing could change that. He didn't want to change it. To hell with the divorce, he just didn't think any judge had the power to undo what God had done. Grover Layton thought the same. Jack had visited the preacher in his office one day and more or less told him about himself.

"I'm a sinner," he said.

"We're all sinners."

"I know I'm pretty bad."

"Don't glory in it, son. And don't think you can do anything about it by yourself. There's only one way to get out of the clutches of the devil."

He would have given a full-fledged sermon then and there if Jack hadn't said he had to go. As near as he could figure out, he was a sinner whether he repented or not. Not that he was criticizing. What Grover Layton said made as much sense as anything else. He did have a preference for the Old Testament though.

He told Louise he'd meet her at the truckstop. "Go into the restaurant. I'll meet you there."

"What time?"

"This afternoon."

"What time this afternoon?"

"I work all day."

She said she'd be there at one and he told her make it two, figuring it would be less crowded. They could get a booth. He didn't want to sit at the counter and have Bonnie hanging around and wondering what was going on. Jack wondered himself.

"What's the message?"

Louise wasn't bad looking, what there was of her, little runt of a woman, but big tits. She pulled her coat sweater tighter when Jack concentrated on them. He remembered her out in her yard, in the summer, wearing a breech clout and bra, sipping iced tea and looking around with big sunglasses. A woman waiting for something to happen. Apparently it never did.

"Message?"

"Did Ellen send you?"

"No! She doesn't know I'm here." She moved her knee when he pressed against it. She leaned forward, forgetting about clutching her coat sweater. "It's about Tommy."

Jack said nothing but a hard knot formed in his stomach while he waited.

"He's a very brilliant boy, as I don't have to tell you, and in a way this is none of my business, and I wouldn't be here if I hadn't found out quite by accident when Ellen took me in to see his chemistry lab, the one in his room, and that's when I saw it."

"What?" Calm, calm, he wanted to reach across the table and grab her by the throat. Spit it out, for God's sake.

"He had a human skull in his room."

She whispered it, one word at a time, looking around before and after. Jack could have shouted with relief. He had been prepared for bad news, real bad news, and all this nosy bitch had to tell him was that Tommy had a skull in his room.

"He's got the whole skeleton. We bought it for him."

She shook this away. "I know about that. This was a real skull. It's gone now, but the skeleton still has one."

"I took it back," Jack said, and Louise shut up, her mouth half open, staring at him. "I gave it to him but I took it back. I'm an Indian giver."

"Is it real?" The words seemed squeezed out of her.

"It's my father."

He laughed but she didn't know whether to take it as

a joke or not. Jack figured she'd seen something Tommy
had ordered through the mail the way they had the
skeleton.

"Let's talk about you."

"Me?"

"You're quite a woman, Louise. I always envied
Wallace."

"Willis."

"Him too. All of them."

She tried to frown, but then she smiled. "You're
awful."

"You only get to grade me afterward."

It was idle joshing mainly, except that Jack had the
feeling that Louise could be had easily. All she had to do
was overcome her fear.

"I've got to go."

"It's right over there."

"That isn't what I meant."

His knee was pressed firmly against hers now and
she didn't move. He had the engine out of a White truck
over in the garage or he might have found out what
Louise really had in mind when she called him.

"I've got to go," she said again.

"Keep in touch." He jiggled her knee a little with his
own and finally she stood and got out of the booth.

"I thought you ought to know. I thought it was
important."

"I appreciate it, Louise. I really do."

He watched her hurry to the door and outside before
getting out of the booth.

"Who was that?" Bonnie asked in a flat voice.

"She didn't say."

"You sonofabitch."

ELEVEN

Andrew was out when Jerome Blatz came so Susannah showed him in to Gerald's office. Blatz was the kind of client Gerald felt least prepared to deal with. The guy looked like a hick, he acted like a hick, but he was a millionaire. A poor mouth millionaire. Andrew had explained to Gerald that farmers never had good years, the times were always bad, they never admitted making a profit.

"It's superstition," Andrew had explained. "Once you admit you're making money, you'll go broke. All they claim they want is parity."

"What's that?"

"It's what the farmer would earn if the laws of the market did not apply. Government aid is based on it. Industrial farmers love it."

Now Jerome ran the tips of his fingers along the bill of his cap, like a pitcher about to throw a spitball.

"Andrew find out why they want my land?"

"Oh, it's not just yours, Mr. Blatz. They've talked with others."

"I know that."

"What we don't know is whether they want all four pieces of land, or just the one they can get the best deal on."

"Who else are they after besides Bink Philips? The reason I ask is I got an idea. If we band together, act as a group, Andrew representing us, we stand a better chance of making the best deal."

"That's a good idea."

"You should have thought of it."

"Andrew already did."

Blatz tucked in his chin and his eyes disappeared under the shade of his cap.

"He explained to me that the drawbacks outweigh the advantages."

Gerald couldn't very well tell Jerome that Andrew thought any alliance between Blatz and Philips would be entered into by each man with the idea of betraying the other. And adding Wendell Jensen would only increase the opportunity for deception.

"I might as well try to act in concert with McGough," Andrew had said.

"You might talk to him, lawyer to lawyer," Gerald said.

Andrew turned away from the suggestion, literally, frowning over Wyler. "You find out anything else?"

He meant from Julie. Not that he would say so. Julie was tainted because Frank McGough was her father and Andrew had vetoed in an absolutely humorless way Gerald's interest in her.

"He can't be serious," Gerald said to Susannah. Susannah had been Andrew's administrative assistant before becoming his wife, his second wife, and the less said about the first the better.

"He married her because she had been going with Frank."

"Come on."

"It's true."

"Is that what he has against McGough?"

Susannah had a nice laugh. Gerald had suggested they record it and use it instead of door chimes. She seemed to approve of Gerald's interest in Julie, but what married woman does not approve of a single man's running the risk of marriage? Risk wasn't the word that occurred to Gerald in the privacy of his own mind, where he frequently debated the matter of Julie.

He had tried to find out more from her about her father's mysterious client but she had bristled. "Will you quit pumping me? I have a very limited knowledge of Daddy's practice but even if I knew all about it, I couldn't tell you and you shouldn't ask."

"You're right."

"Of course I'm right."

He let her enjoy her victory. She put a hand on his.

"What if I kept pressing you with questions about your uncle Andrew?"

"You wouldn't."

"Of course I wouldn't. If he wants to know things about Mr. Blatz and Mr. Philips, he should ask them."

"Who are they?"

She gave him a look. "The men whose land you've been asking me about. Have they leagued together?"

"Would it help?"

She did say that if the land purchase went through it would be of great benefit to Wyler, but Andrew considered the remark to be worthless.

"She doesn't know anything," Andrew concluded. "Frank wouldn't confide even in his own daughter."

"Where is Andrew?" Jerome Blatz asked now in Gerald's office. His tone was querulous and he jiggled his foot as if his bladder was giving him trouble.

"Seeing a priest."

That shut up Jerome, at least for a moment. Gerald told the farmer Andrew could be back at any moment.

"Then again . . ." He let his voice trail away. "But you're welcome to wait."

"I'll wait."

"Good." Gerald stood. "You'll be more comfortable in the other room. Susannah can give you coffee."

"Are you trying to get rid of me?"

"I don't want my uncle to think I'm trying to steal his client."

In the doorway, Jerome stopped and tipped back his head to look up at Gerald. "Andrew isn't even Catholic."

"That's right."

"So why's he seeing a priest?"

"Confidential."

Andrew had gone to St. Luke's to talk with Father Foley about the likely effects of the pending legislation outlawing bingo. Across the state there was a groundswell of protest. The state lottery was a fixture now and there was even talk of permitting gambling on waterways, following the lead of Illinois.

"I don't think Foley has a thing to worry about," Andrew had said.

His reason was that the local state senator was numbered among the anti-gambling forces in Indianapolis. "Boyd Carlson has an instinct for losing causes. My guess is that the whole bingo flap is meant to create sympathy for expanded gambling."

That was the message Andrew had carried to Father Foley at St. Luke's. Gerald had taken Julie to the parish hall on Wednesday night, or she had taken him; after all, it was her parish. It hadn't provided the same anonymity as the revival chapel but Gerald had won and Julie had lost. Theirs was a competitive relationship. Maybe they would check out the bingo parlor run by Clark Cooper and his wife at the Bison Bar. Andrew intended to reassure them as well. There might not be a consortium of farmers whose land was coveted by a Chicago purchaser, but those who ran bingo games intended to band together.

TWELVE

In eighth grade Phillipa had given a classroom pre-
sentation on Ralph Nader, a fateful event. From that
moment on, she had found her mission in life. Like the
famous crusader, she felt called on to address the great
and small injustices of the world. Unlike her model,
however, she was not interested in her fellow citizens as
consumers. The struggle to get big business to respond
to the real or imaginary grievances of their customers
was insufficient to address the idealism in Phillipa's
soul. Her concern was with people as people. And her
preference, though she would not have said so even if
she were aware of it, was lost causes.

When she began to live with Clark Cooper, it had
been more therapeutic than romantic. He was drinking
then and she felt a call deep within herself to reform
him. The ease with which he got drunk was the source
of her guess that he had Indian blood. She assured him
that it was a scientific fact that the Irish and the

American Indians were physiologically susceptible to alcoholism.

"Maybe I'm Irish."

That was a possibility to be excluded first of all. Phillipa herself was more Irish than English and less English than Welsh and she knew all about drinking from her own family. Her father drank, her uncles drank, and now her brothers drank. No wonder she herself was a teetotaler. She had done research on Clark sufficient to convince herself that it was not Irish blood that explained his weakness in the matter of liquor. The same research—and talking with Bonnie, his sister—had convinced her that Clark was one sixty-fourth Indian, most likely a minuscule tribe that had been all but absorbed by the Miami. She preferred to think of the tribe as Clark's extended family. The discovery excited her in a way she did not at first understand. And then the realization came. She was meant to devote her life drawing attention to the injustices done Native Americans.

"Marry me," she said to Clark.

He had a broad flat face on which his nose sat as if hastily puttied on and his ebony eyes seemed never to blink. Phillipa found it easy to imagine his ancestors staring out over the unravaged plains of the continent, leading a simple nomadic life before the advent of the white man. Just living with him did not suffice to connect her to that noble past. She wanted marriage.

"A tribal ceremony," she explained.

She had done research on tribal customs and ceremonies at the Wyler Historical Society under the mildly disapproving eye of Earl Sanders, the curator. Out of unconscious caution, she developed a hybrid account of Clark's background, borrowing from the lore of various tribes that had populated the Midwest before they were driven out by the white man. Instinctively, she wanted to avoid appropriation by or objections from those tribes whose history was well established and whose members might oppose the project that was vaguely forming in her mind.

"Who'll conduct the ceremony?" Clark wondered.

"You do, basically. And I have things to do as well. The others just witness what we are doing."

He didn't like it. Bonnie thought she was nuts.

"Marry him in front of a justice of the peace or a judge first, then do the Indian thing."

Bonnie was right. Undisputed legal status had its attractions. But Clark was not at all taken with the idea of a legal wedding.

"What would it change? We've got a life."

Well, they did as long as he kept away from alcohol. He tried. At least he stopped drinking under her vigilance, but she never had the sense that he himself was convinced he ought to stop. That was indispensable. It was something she had learned working with addicts.

Her roommates in Urbana had smoked pot in the apartment and sometimes Phillipa felt the secondary effects of the smoke-filled air. This sent her off on a solitary jog along the campus paths. She was mystified by the desire to drug oneself into oblivion. What pleasure could match that of a clear mind, the sting of fresh air in the lungs as she ran, ahead a whole world to be cherished and healed? After graduation, she did volunteer work in a rehab center, then turned her attention to the homeless. She had first visited Wyler when she returned a local girl to her family, driving her from Chicago where the teenager had been on an almost fatal downspin. In Wyler, Phillipa stopped by a local soup kitchen—all her holidays were busman's holidays—and met Clark.

They talked, he was profoundly drunk and full of self-pity but, she sensed, wanted to escape from his habit. She found it impossible to just leave him. She would have been haunted ever afterward by the thought that he had drunk himself to death after her departure. She could not leave Wyler until she was certain all was well with him.

She never left. They slept together for days before it meant anything other than sharing her bed with him. One morning she woke up and he was on top of her and it seemed only another favor she could do him. Under her guidance, using his veterans' benefits, he bought the Bison Bar. A mobile home behind the tavern came with it and that is where they lived. Proximity to alcohol would innoculate him psychologically, that was her theory. The bingo too was her suggestion, a kind of down payment on the hope that she could get him out of the tavern business entirely.

His resistance to a legal wedding made him willing to go through the Indian ceremony she had devised during her studies at the Wyler Historical Society. The witnesses were in various stages of sobriety, but it didn't matter. Moving slowly and with dignity through the ritual of fertility, Phillipa felt that she was reclaiming a former self that had been Native American through and through.

Her excitement and dedication survived the bad times when Clark fell off the wagon and started to drink again. He was abusive to her, of course, drunks are usually abusive. Phillipa defended herself as well as she could, locked her door to him, and waited out the tempest. She became an expert at tracking the phases of his alcoholic periods. His body soon reacted to the toxic excess, she nursed him through the first bad time of recovery, she turned his remorse and self-disgust to good purpose. And, when he became particularly menacing, she held him at bay with the rifle she took down from over his desk and carried out to their mobile home whenever he began to drink.

The campaign to close down bingo had affected Clark strangely. Sometimes she thought he secretly wished he'd be driven from his semirespectable life so he could sink into the gutter again, able to blame "them" for what had happened. It was something she had learned about society's victims—they came to accept, almost to cherish, their fallen condition. This was why help was resisted, sometimes subtly, sometimes violently, as if the offer to lift them up was an assault on their identity. Phillipa understood how Ralph Nader had been baffled by automobile manufacturers, unable to understand them, unable too to understand the willingness of people to be exploited. Phillipa's work among the downtrodden had taught her many truths about the human animal, most of them unintelligible.

Today she sat in her usual place in the Wyler Historical Society building, a converted firehouse. A brass pole rose from the floor and went on up into the second floor where Earl Sanders had his office. From time to time, Phillipa would become aware of him looking down at her.

Earl was a curator who preferred to have the things in his care unused, if his treatment of her was any indication. It was only with reluctance that he had given her access to the little he had on the Indians who had lived in this area before the coming of the white settlers. At her insistence, he added more things, most of it printed and standard, yet still important.

"The library should be ordering these things."

"I suppose most of what you have here could be said to belong in a library."

That pointed remark, plus a mild suggestion that protests against the anti-Native American prejudice of the WHS might be in the offing, loosened him up some-what, though she knew he never really approved of the line she took.

Today she had come to the WHS as to a refuge. Clark was in the first wild phase of a new drinking bout and she did not want to think of the Bison Bar and Bingo Parlor, she wanted to scrub from her mind all memories of her life since she had come to Wyler. She hoped bingo would be banned. She sat there wishing she had never heard of or seen this Indiana town.

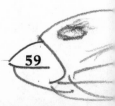

59

THIRTEEN

After six years in the assembly, Boyd Carlson had moved up to the senate where he was now in his fourth term. He had reached a crossroads of his political career. To remain in state politics, to rise to the role of minority leader, was not an ignoble ideal, but it was not for that that Boyd Carlson had put his insurance company in neutral, in his wife Wendy's charge for a third of the year at least. All he asked was that she wouldn't lose any business, but of course he couldn't say it out loud. The responsibility had raised her consciousness and when she said she had taken the business in new directions she meant to be understood positively. He stifled the urge to explain to her that success and a dwindling income do not accompany one another. Wendy had developed a theory about the social responsibilities of the Carlson Insurance Agency, the idea picked up from a sermon at St. Luke's. It seemed another reason to shut down Father Foley's bingo business. And perhaps to retire from politics and concentrate on rebuilding his agency. At the beginning of the current legislative session he had returned to his Indianapolis hotel room, stood in front of the bathroom mirror, and studied the man whose party had just denied him a leadership role. It was a bitter moment. He felt like resigning then and there. But it had been the darkest moment before the light shone through. By light he meant Mankowitz, the lobbyist who was waiting for him in the hotel lobby when he came down for dinner.

"Got time for a drink?"

Boyd looked toward the ill-lit cavern off the lobby from which sounds of music and laughter drifted. It was a place he had avoided throughout his legislative years. Mankowitz took his elbow and steered him into the bar. Why not? He had half a mind to get a six-pack and drink it all in solitude in his room. To hell with politics.

"What's the occasion?" he asked Mankowitz. Once they were settled in a booth, he could hardly make out the other man's face. A waitress in a black mesh outfit that clung to her body appeared. "Bourbon," Mankowitz said and Boyd said "Ditto."

"I want to make a significant contribution to your reelection campaign."

"I've been asking myself if I'll run again."

"Oh, you have to."

"No I don't. I'm going broke."

"And you weren't elected to the leadership."

Their drinks came. "Cheers," Boyd said gloomily and tried his drink. He almost never drank liquor.

"I have a proposal."

Mankowitz said he spoke for an informal conglomerate interested in having existing laws on bingo enforced and new and tougher ones passed. Bingo? In the past, Mankowitz had sought his vote for tax breaks for new industry, for labor legislation, for help on legislative odds and ends. He seemed to be a floating lobbyist, picking up clients as occasions arose. He was serious about bingo.

"Your problem, Carlson, is that you need a cause. A crusade. This may be it. We think it is and we want to work with you."

They had another bourbon and when they went into the restaurant for their dinner they might have been old allies. By not rejecting the proposal, Boyd had accepted it. Why not? After a defeat, he was being offered the opportunity to make an end run around the party. And bingo as a cause was squeaky clean. The possibilities for righteous oratory were infinite. Mankowitz nodded.

"It's what attracts me too."

After the muscle he had exerted on behalf of the unionization of state workers? Boyd had opposed that. Mankowitz's tactics on behalf of the union had been intense, embarrassing to proponents of the legislation, annoying to Boyd. Bingo made them bedfellows.

"Frank McGough suggested I speak to you, Boyd."

"About this?"

"He is a major contributor to the campaign."

Boyd checked that out with McGough. He had feared that his failure to get elected to a leadership post would alienate his chief financial contributor. McGough was indeed behind the anti-bingo drive.

In the first weeks of the effort, Boyd worried that he had made a mistake. There was joshing from fellow senators on the floor and off, the leadership looked askance at his free-lance endeavors, political cartoons showed him dressed as a Puritan, Wendy called and said she couldn't believe her ears.

"Do you know what bingo means to St. Luke's?"

"What they're already doing is arguably against existing laws."

"Then you should be trying to get those laws off the books, not adding new ones."

He listened to her, feeling that he was several thousand feet above her, elevated by the support of Mankowitz and his cohorts, chief among them McGough. Boyd had checked out the group and his sense of having found his destiny increased. With this kind of backing, who knew how far he might go?

Alas, Wendy's demur about St. Luke's was only the beginning of opposition from his constituents. Everybody became a constituent when they had a beef, whether they had voted for you or not. That didn't seem fair. Father Foley called him in and as much as ordered him to desist from opposing bingo.

"Don't forget the separation of church and state, Father."

"Oh, I'll separate the church if that's what you want. I'll separate every vote in this parish, and many others besides. People will go on playing bingo whatever the law is. Think of Prohibition."

"That's exactly what I'm thinking of."

"The Volstead Act," Foley said and, when Boyd still didn't understand, explained it in terms he was sure his senator would understand. "Elliot Ness and the Untouchables, man."

He heard from Clark Cooper and his wife as well, a petition six feet long filled with signatures of alleged constituents. Humphrey Ward at the *Dealer* had him in for what he called an editorial conference. "You're on the wrong side on this one, Boyd," Humphrey said, every bit as officious as Foley had been.

"Drop it," Wendy advised. "Get out while you can and repudiate the bill."

"I can't do that."

"Why?"

"Frank McGough."

That quieted Wendy. McGough was Boyd's principal backer in the district, not just in words, as in the case of Humphrey and the *Dealer*, but in sizable direct and indirect contributions to Boyd's reelection war chest. One Frank McGough made up for a regiment of bingo players. Nonetheless, Boyd went around to see the lawyer and tell him of the opposition that was building up against him.

"Forget the critics. You're on the winning side."

"What do you have against bingo?"

The question surprised McGough. What did he think they were talking about? But then he said, "It's against the law and I'm a lawyer."

He half expected McGough to wink or laugh when he said that. But if it was meant as a joke, McGough gave no indication of the fact. "Carlson, I see a great future for you in politics."

Wendy raised her brows and nodded when he quoted the remark to her. She no longer nagged him to abandon the anti-bingo crusade. If nothing else, Boyd Carlson had become a household name across the state. He was featured in the Indianapolis papers, ambiguously endorsed in South Bend, cursed in Gary. Political cartoons grew vicious. Humphrey held the *Wyler Dealer* to a neutral position, not wanting to antagonize either Frank McGough or Andrew Broom.

Boyd himself felt suffused with righteousness. He refused an invitation to appear in Grover Layton's pulpit at the tabernacle but he knew that his name was in good odor with the preacher. Layton's accusation that forces in the Vatican were using bingo to undermine the moral fiber of the nation suggested the dangers in his new alliances.

FOURTEEN

Father Foley seemed more upset by the fact that Boyd Carlson was a Catholic than that he was in the vanguard of those seeking to outlaw bingo.

"Never trust a Catholic politician," Father Foley said to Andrew Broom. His skin was the color of strawberries, his thick wavy hair going gray—and there were squint lines at the corners of his eyes. He had the look of a man who laughed easily but he was angry now. "I speak in confidence, of course."

"Of course."

"It's his wife that's Catholic. He came into the Church when they married. I wonder if it really took." He might have been carrying on a conversation with himself but then he seemed to remember that Susannah was a parishioner at St. Luke's. She was at Mass when Andrew was on the golf course. Father Foley's eyes rolled heavenward. "God forgive me."

Foley was sixty, a widowed grandfather who had

65

entered the seminary when he was fifty and been a priest only half a dozen years.

"I didn't know a married man could become a priest," Andrew said.

"I was a widower. There are several seminaries for retarded vocations." Foley's smile came out like the sun from behind a cloud. "We were all of an age, half had been married and lost their wives, airline pilots, chemists, two plumbers, teachers galore. It was an odd four years but I survived."

"What did you do before?"

Foley looked over both shoulders with exaggerated caution. "I was a dentist."

Did Susannah know all this about her pastor? Foley had been given St. Luke's when the previous pastor went on leave of absence, which, Foley assured Andrew, was a euphemism. "Did you know the man, Mr. Broom?"

"I met him, yes."

"I never did. People try to talk to me about him, but I don't allow it. Speak well of former pastors, as the poet says."

Foley seemed far more of a priest than Barker had. The bingo had started with the change of pastors and within months St. Luke's had a popular and successful Wednesday night bingo that ran from six until ten. Foley intended to get the parish out from under the debt Barker had built up as quickly as he could.

"We think of it as a town event as much as a parish function."

That seemed right to Andrew. Foley was not wholly reassured by Andrew's interpretation of what lay behind the proposed ban on bingo.

"It's a diversionary tactic, Father. They attack bingo, there is a popular uproar, and in the wake of that they put through legalized gambling."

"But what if they succeed in shutting down bingo?"

Boyd Carlson's speeches on the subject might have been delivered from a pulpit. His tack was that he and his cohorts in the legislature were trying to help good Christians live by their own principles. The fact that Carlson thought gambling was incompatible with Christianity was the basis for Foley's suspicion that Boyd's conversion to Catholicism had been only superficial.

From St. Luke's Andrew drove to the lower end of town where Clark Cooper and his wife ran a combination saloon and bingo parlor. That he could spend as much time as he did away from the office, involved in the great and small affairs of Wyler, was the main attraction of his remaining here, and it gratified Andrew that his nephew Gerald fitted in so well. He felt he had saved the boy from the well-paid drudgery of a big-city firm. Not at a financial sacrifice, of course. He had matched the highest offer Gerald had received when he brought him to Wyler, he treated him as an equal partner, and Gerald was, somber thought, his only heir after Susannah. Money did not isolate a person in a town this size and that was good. The size of the town and the easygoing democracy of its citizens had the bad effect that it was difficult to avoid people too. Frank McGough, his old nemesis, was an all-too-frequent presence.

"Andrew, you have next to nothing to do with him. Why let him bother you so?"

"Bother me? He doesn't bother me at all."

"Of course he doesn't."

He smiled. A wife should be the one person you cannot fool. That fit Susannah as it had not Dorothy. The fooling had gone in the opposite direction with Dorothy.

However generally true Susannah's remark that he had little to do with Frank McGough, it was not true in either the land purchase offers or in the squabble over bingo. He and Frank were ranged on opposite sides on both. Would Andrew have risen to the defense of bingo otherwise? As for the McGough client who was interested in land along the Tippecanoe, Andrew had just decided that whatever project was intended it would not help the town.

The part of town in which the Bison Bar and Bingo Parlor was located had benefited from well-conceived and well-executed restoration work over the past decade, but the Bison was a reminder of what it had been like before. The long low building had escaped the planning commission's attention largely because it was nestled on the riverbank below the train station, concealed from view, an eyesore that had to be sought out in order to give offense. Its unpaved parking lot was rutted and scored with the tire tracks of patrons. That lot was a sea of mud when it rained and that explained the boot scraper Andrew nearly tripped on before entering the dimly lit beery interior of the Bison.

In mid-afternoon, the place was all but deserted. Two men sat at a small round table on the edge of what must serve as a dance floor on the evenings it wasn't filled with folding tables for bingo. Music of the 1950s, Rosemary Clooney singing "Come On-a My House" was succeeded by Guy Mitchell as Andrew crossed to the bar. The man behind the bar watched him warily as he approached.

"Where's Mr. Cooper?"

"Clark?"

"That's right."

"You can leave a message."

To the left of the bar was a closed door marked office. Andrew went to it and knocked. The bartender protested, "Hey. He's trying to get some rest."

The door did not open, the bartender glared at him.

He could of course leave, but that might suggest to the bartender that the decision was due to him. Andrew banged on the door more forcefully and it swung inward. The bartender was jabbering disapproval when Andrew stepped into the office.

The room was empty. The bartender seemed genuinely surprised. "He must be out back."

Out back was a mobile home. It had been painted a bilious yellow and seemed sunk into its flat tires, but there were jacks under both ends to lend it stability. Andrew felt he could topple the thing with a good shove. He knocked on the flimsy sheet metal door and turned the handle. It was unlocked. He pushed it open.

Clark Cooper lay just inside making it impossible to open the door completely. There was a frown on his face and from his open mouth discordant sounds and lethal breath emerged.

FIFTEEN

Ellen answered the door and Jack felt as flustered as he had on their first date when he realized how different she was, that this was one he might marry. Today, come to see Tommy, he had not waited in the car as he usually did until Tommy came out. If he leaned over into the passenger seat, he could look up at the house and see Ellen in the window, watching her son run out to his father. Jack was filled with guilt at the way he had destroyed his family. Ellen had been right to divorce him, he admitted that now. By all rights he ought to keep away from them, let Tommy be brought up decently by his mother. The older Tommy got, the more Jack worried that the kid would turn out like him. It had been a long time since he had seen Ellen this close. She seemed as pure and good as a statue in a church.

"Tommy home?"

"No."

There was just the locked screen door between them and he felt the power of her presence. He looked away, then at his feet before looking directly at her through the mesh.

"I know this isn't my day. Where is he?"

"Out." His expression made her add, "He doesn't always tell me where he's going. And I don't ask."

He moved his face closer to the screen. "Can I come in?" He was whispering and his eyes flicked in the direction of the house next door. Her hand seemed to have a mind of its own. Her finger flipped up the hook and eye lock, and she pushed open the door. He slipped inside.

"Louise," he said.

"What about Louise?"

"I suppose she saw me come to the door but maybe not. Ellen, she called me up and said she wanted to talk."

"Louise!"

"She said she saw something in Tommy's room and then when she came snooping around on her own it was gone."

"A skull." Ellen said it with contempt.

"Where is it?"

"I told him to get rid of it and he did."

"I'd like to talk with him."

"You're supposed to come every other Saturday."

He hadn't come for his son for a month but he'd phoned and lied about being busy. Did Tommy even care?

"When did Louise come see you?"

"I don't trust that woman," Jack said.

"What do you mean?"

How could he tell Ellen about pressing his knee against Louise's at the truckstop, certain that if he'd been free he could have been making love to her within five minutes? How close was Ellen to the neighbor woman now? Jack didn't like the idea of outside influence on the woman to whom he still felt married, before God, but now, seeing her, he rejected the suspicion.

Ellen was above that kind of thing, she always had been. He had the almost welcome thought that he'd done her a favor when he gave her reason to get rid of him.

Louise had only been an excuse. Jack wanted a look in Tommy's room and Ellen let him. "I've told you though, it's no longer there."

The skull. There was that goddam skeleton doing a bony dance in a corner of the room, the wire from which it hung from the ceiling invisible. What a kid. Jack felt a wave of paternal affection sweep over him. Why hadn't he changed when he married Ellen, become what a husband is supposed to be, faithful and dependable? Tommy should have sealed the bargain, his own son, a kid he wanted to grow up to be . . . What? He didn't even know and, given the grades Tommy got in school, his future could be anything.

Shelves filled with books and jars, the lab in the corner, on the wall a team picture of the Minnesota Twins. The rack over the bed was empty, the fishing rod gone. Jack now had a good idea where he could find his son.

He turned to Ellen and shook his head. "He must get it from you, Ellen."

She said nothing. What could she say? Tommy looked like him but that better be the end of it. Jack didn't want his son turning into an ass hound like his old man.

"I do worry about him, Jack."

"Why?" They went back into the living room, where Jack stood by the door, ready to go.

"There are drugs being sold at school now."

Her expression was concerned but that was all. Nonetheless Jack felt that she was pointing a finger at him. Nothing Grover Layton could say about the world going to hell in a hand basket could prevent the hard knot of guilty terror from forming in Jack's stomach.

"I wish you'd talk to him about things like that, Jack."

"I came here hoping I could."

"Come on Saturday like you're supposed to."

He nodded, opened the door, and before stepping out looked around the once familiar room that now seemed to represent something from which he was forever separated.

"Saturday," he said.

In his car, he headed for the river. That's where he had taken Tommy fishing and the missing rod suggested that's where the boy was.

This unscheduled visit had been prompted by things falling together in his mind when he was in bed with Bonnie, arms behind his head, staring at the ceiling while she jabbered. Her crazy sister-in-law encouraged Clark to exploit his supposed Indian heritage.

"You ought to tell him your father was out West at the time he was conceived."

"I told Phillipa. She just laughed. She thinks I'm lying. She says she's located the possible Indian burying ground and her new campaign is to claim it for her people."

"Her people through Clark who ain't Indian?"

"That woman could have been a preacher."

"You ever listen to Grover Layton?"

"The phony healer?"

"Don't say that."

"What should I say?"

"Please."

Her mouth widened in a smile and she moved toward him, nuzzling against his chest. He removed a hand from behind his head and laid it on her hair. He pressed down, feeling the bone beneath. Her skull. Tommy. Phillipa's campaign about the Indian burial ground. The skull. It was the line he'd inhaled that made his mind so clear. Suddenly he saw it all. His son had stumbled on those grounds and Jack wanted to know where they were.

Tommy was nowhere in sight where they had often

fished, where there was public access to the river. Jack scouted around, looked through the little stand of woods where he noticed some leaves that seemed to have been made into a pile. He kicked them away. The ground had been dug into and not too long ago. With the toe of his work shoe he kicked away enough dirt to uncover the plastic bag. The skull was inside. He felt like a grave robber. Tommy might have returned the thing but he hadn't taken much trouble to conceal where he had hidden it.

Jack took the plastic bag back to his car and put it into the trunk. He was driving away before he realized that he hadn't taken much of a look at the river.

SIXTEEN

Andrew learned from Humphrey Ward that McGough was indeed behind the odd crusade on which Boyd Carlson had embarked. It made no sense. Andrew was as little attracted to gambling as he was to its suppression. Susannah's suggestion that they drive to Illinois and spend a day gambling and dining on one of the boats now plying the Mississippi, seeking to separate citizens from their money, left him cold.

"You're kidding."

"Gerald loved it. He drove to Galena and had a wonderful time."

"With whom?"

She tipped her head and looked at him. He must learn not to expect sympathy from Susannah in his effort to keep Gerald and Julie McGough apart.

"A law school classmate who drove down from Chicago."

Male or female? Better let it go. It would be a relief if Gerald fell in love with someone other than Julie. Of course that might carry problems of its own. Would a classmate ensconced in Chicago be amenable to a move to Wyler? What a Hobson's choice that would be: Gerald in Wyler but smitten by Julie or Gerald in Chicago free of Julie but, alas, no longer the heir apparent of his uncle Andrew's law firm.

Susannah dealt brochures onto the breakfast table, glossy publications featuring paddlewheelers suggestive of an earlier day. These were the floating casinos to which Illinois politicians had turned in the hope of funding their follies.

"Sweetheart, I consider state lotteries an abomination. I always associated them with backward countries, Latin American dictatorships, Turkey—one slender hope to make life tolerable in an impoverished setting."

"Oh don't be a fuddy-dud. I buy lottery tickets. Everyone does."

"I don't."

"That's my point."

Not one reached by logic, apparently. Andrew let it go. He had no wish to quarrel with his lovely wife. The thought of Gerald driving across Illinois to board a state-licensed gambling boat clung to his mind and not because his nephew would have risked losing some money. If Susannah could be believed Gerald had returned several hundred dollars to the good.

"Why Galena?"

Susannah made an impatient sound and began to open one of the brochures. "But why there? Illinois now has legalized gambling on all its waterways."

And then the thought came, all at once, whole. Recent events interlocked and took on collective meaning. Of course! McGough was representing Chicago clients in local real estate ventures, Boyd Carlson was McGough's creature. To deprive the citizens of Indiana of the innocent pastime of bingo would create a backlash that could lead to the legalization of gambling in the state. Soon, as in Illinois, Hoosier waterways would be plied by gambling boats. That seemed the explanation of Boyd's otherwise quixotic campaign against bingo.

"What's so funny?"

"Funny?"

"You're smiling."

"I just got your point about the lottery," he lied.

They drove to the office in separate cars. After parking, Andrew walked over to the *Dealer* where he found Humphrey in a yoga position in the corner of his office, eyes closed, palms pressed firmly together. What in the world was happening to Wyler, Indiana?

"Shangri-la," Andrew whispered.

Humphrey's eyes half-opened, then shut again.

"Boyd Carlson is acting as agent for Illinois gambling interests."

Humphrey unwound and stood, rolled up his mat, and went to his desk. His eyes flicked to the painting of his mother but Andrew felt he already had old Mrs. Ward's support.

"What do you mean?"

It sounded even better as he developed the idea for Humphrey. That Boyd Carlson had become the leader of the anti-bingo crusade was simply a matter of fact. What was obscure to an extreme was why. If one had imagined an opinion on bingo for the state senator, it would have been pro, if only because of his connection with St. Luke's. Why had he betrayed his parish, antagonized his constituents, invited ridicule? Clearly principle had nothing to do with it. So what was his interest?

"The net effect of banning bingo in Indiana will be to increase the pool of people likely to favor legalized gambling."

"Boyd maintains that bingo is against laws already on the books."

"No judge has ever agreed with him. Which is no doubt why he proposes new and draconian laws."

"Draconian?"

"How many bingo players do you know?"

"Do you play?"

"Go down to St. Luke's some Wednesday night."

Humphrey did not agree even after forty-five minutes of discussion that the *Dealer* owed it to its readers to expose the perfidy of their senator.

"I know you've supported him in the past, Humphrey. That doesn't mean he owns you."

"Nobody owns the *Dealer*."

"You do. That gives you dangerous power. Arbitrary power. Here's a chance to assure your readers that you retain your independence."

Humphrey promised to investigate the matter and see if there was any substance to Andrew's speculative charge. Andrew walked whistling back to the Hoosier Towers. He felt that he had struck a blow against Frank McGough, however oblique. Perhaps only Susannah and Humphrey and Frank McGough himself would know, but that was more than enough. All Andrew asked of a move against Frank was that Frank knew. Any publicity was a bonus.

Jerome Blatz, Bink Philips, and Wendell Jensen, without an appointment, were waiting for him in his office.

"We've decided to sell."

"All of you?"

The trio exchanged mistrustful looks. Jerome seemed to be their spokesman. "We want to make a package deal. My land, Bink's and Wendell's. That way we won't be underselling one another."

Meaning they didn't trust one another not to make a separate deal with Frank McGough and his clients.

"You sure they want all the land."

"It's all or nothing," Wendell said. All for one and one for all? Wendell seemed to be trying to convince himself.

"That makes sense," Andrew conceded. "You talked to Frank McGough?"

"You're our lawyer."

"And this office will be honored to represent the entity you three have decided to become."

The land owners seemed unsure they liked this description of their deed. Bink said they wanted Andrew to get right at it. He picked up the phone and asked Susannah to make an appointment with Frank McGough. The trio rose, satisfied, and Andrew went with them to the elevator. He wanted to make sure they left.

"I want Gerald to keep that appointment."

"Millie said that John Lindel would see you."

Lindel was a nephew of Mrs. McGough. When the young man arrived in Wyler, Andrew had seen his advent as a typical McGough move, aping Andrew's acquisition of Gerald. It seemed fitting that the two young men should represent the old antagonists who would not willingly meet.

SEVENTEEN

Lindel squatted to put his tee in the ground, set his ball upon it like a magician balancing a plate on a stick, then straddled the earth like a nervous Colossus as he waggled the club head of his driver. He cocked his eye at the ball and lunged, bending his elbow on his backswing, hit the ball. It went like a taut rope six feet off the ground two hundred yards out into the fairway.

"Shit," said Lindel.

"Good drive," Gerald said, but his partner for the day was examining his grip to discover the explanation for his supposedly poor performance.

Gerald teed up, addressed the ball, swung easily. His ball described a rising arc, hooking slightly, landed beyond Lindel's and continued on another forty yards.

"You use a metal wood?" Lindel asked when, side by side in the cart, they headed out onto the fairway. Gerald said he did. "That's the difference," Lindel said.

It was not an auspicious beginning. Meeting for golf so that they could discuss matters of mutual interest

(Andrew's phrase) had not been Gerald's suggestion. Nor Andrew's either. Indeed, his uncle had frowned when Gerald told him of Lindel's proposal.

"What's his handicap?"

"I don't know."

When asked, Lindel had replied that he was sound of wind and limb, but the pleasantry was not prelude to anything further. Andrew's frown deepened.

"He sounds like a sandbagger to me."

"We'll just play even Stephen."

"You ever see him on the course?"

Gerald was not sure he had ever seen McGough's nephew on or off the course. Susannah's description did not help. But then it seemed that she had not seen the boy for years.

"Boy?"

"He's about your age."

It was with mixed feelings, accordingly, that Gerald had driven to the course in Plymouth that Lindel suggested. The club was a public one, Lindel was unprepossessing in running shoes, a sweater pulled over a dress shirt, suit pants. Andrew's suspicion of a sandbagger seemed possible, but the first drive was inconclusive.

"You ever regret joining your uncle's firm in Wyler?" Lindel shouted his words, they seemed to hang in front of his face for a moment, then were whisked over his shoulder by the fairly fresh west wind.

"Do you?"

"Of course. I left a large firm in St. Louis for this."

"Why do you stay?"

"Money." He spelled the word, and its letters whipped over his shoulder one at a time.

Lindel skimmed a three-iron onto the green, the ball running through it to the back fringe, but from there he all but holed out. He tapped in for a par. Gerald pin high in two, three putted. It was a bad beginning.

It got worse. On the second tee, Lindel actually whiffed his drive, but then he connected and the ball went like a bullet until it landed and then bounded forward another fifty yards. Lying two. Gerald easily put his drive past Lindel's ball. Lindel, with a wedge he must have bought in a discount drugstore, lofted his ball onto the green, just past the hole, and backspin brought it neatly back into the hole.

"What's par?" Lindel asked.

"You birdied."

"Is that one under par?"

Gerald nodded, gloom settling over him. If Lindel wasn't a sandbagger he was giving a pretty good imitation of one. Gerald birdied but he was down one. On the fourth tee it began to rain and they sat in a shelter, listening to the pensive piddling on the roof above them.

"Just a shower," Lindel said, clearly eager to go on.

"How much do you know of the offers to purchase land along the Tippecanoe River?"

"They're bonafide offers, a bit more than could be gotten in the open market. I'd advise your clients to accept."

"I'm more interested in your clients."

"Payment would be in cash, certified check. They could be anybody."

"That's what bothers me."

"How so?"

"It matters who is buying up land around Wyler. Strangers. From Chicago?"

"Do you have some kind of litmus test in mind?"

"Chicago has its associations."

"How do you mean?"

"What connection is there between this offer and gambling?"

"Gambling?" Lindel looked as puzzled as he did when he addressed the golf ball. Maybe Frank McGough didn't let his nephew into all his dealings. Gerald spelled out for Lindel Andrew's fears about what was going on.

Three local farmers are independently approached by Frank McGough, representing an out-of-town client or clients, offering to buy parcels of land along the Tippecanoe. Put the parcels together and they amounted to an impressive stretch of river frontage. Located only a few miles west of Wyler, it could be an industrial site, a place where condominiums might be built. For that matter, it could make a magnificent estate for a Chicagoan fed up with the city. Some secrecy might accompany any or all such ventures, but Andrew had a strong hunch that something was wrong.

"Why?"

"He doesn't trust Frank McGough."

"It's mutual."

"Andrew suspects a connection with Boyd Carlson's campaign against bingo."

"I don't follow."

This was the tricky part of the theory. Gerald himself had asked Andrew to go through it several times before he got it. Banning bingo would bring on a backlash of anger, people demanding to gamble if they saw fit. Those of a secular bent would accuse religious leaders of imposing their beliefs on the state, such parishes as St. Luke's would be up in arms at the loss of revenue, the Coopers would chime in with their preposterous claim that there was prejudice against Native Americans behind the ban. The result would be the expansion of the lottery and introduction of legalized gambling. Soon the waterways of Indiana like those of Illinois would be swarming with floating casinos.

"That land along the Tippecanoe is ideal for a docking area." Andrew imagined motels, a restaurant, paddlewheelers standing proudly at the dock, awaiting passengers who could combine nostalgia with gambling.

"Not a bad idea," Lindel said.

"Is that the idea?

"I'll ask Frank."

"Doesn't he confide in you?"

"Confide as in confidence?"

Nice point, but Gerald was now convinced that Lindel really didn't know anything. It would have been a good moment for the rain to increase, forcing the cancellation of their match. But suddenly the sun came out and they went out onto the fourth tee. From that point on, Gerald tore up the course and Lindel's game matched the awkwardness with which he played it. Lindel stopped counting at the twelfth hole.

"It's just a friendly match, right?"

Well, it was hard to feel angry at a golfer as bad as Lindel. Gerald was now prepared to believe that Lindel knew as little about his uncle's business as he did about the game of golf. So these had been wasted hours.

In the locker room, dressing after his shower, Gerald said, "We'll advise our clients against selling unless the identity of the purchaser is divulged. You might tell Mr. McGough that."

EIGHTEEN

Ever since meeting Jack at the truckstop, Louise had been obsessed with thoughts of her neighbor's former husband. She told herself that it was ridiculous for a married woman to go all aflutter because a man pressed his knee against hers, but that insolent pressure seemed to symbolize a wild world from which Louise had cut herself off when she made the mistake of her life by marrying Willis Long. Jack had actually hinted that there were men in her life other than Willis! But they were only fantasy men. Still, it seemed significant that he thought of her that way. The man had lived next door for how many years before leaving? He must have watched her when she wasn't aware of it. Louise liked the thought of Jack Parry's eyes on her as she worked in the yard or lay languorously in the sun out back. Had he lusted after her all those years?

She telephoned the truckstop and asked for him, but the garage transferred her call to the dining room and the dining room routed it back to the garage. The third time a woman in the lunchroom asked who was calling. Louise refused to say.

"He's at the doctor for his treatment."

"What treatment?"

"I'm not sure he'd want you to know."

"But you don't know who I am."

"You got it."

"A friend."

"Jack has lots of friends."

Sure. And Louise bet the woman on the phone wished she were one of them.

"A neighbor."

She hung up. She drove to the truckstop to fill up the car but there was no sign of Jack. What had the woman meant by a treatment at the doctor's? Was he ill? The cashier worked in a little booth between the rows of pumps.

"Do you have Jack Parry's home number?"

The boy squinted at her through the yellowing plexiglass.

"I'm his sister," she added.

"Jack's got lots of sisters."

But he gave her a number, an address, not telephone, and glanced toward the cavern of the garage. Was Jack at work in there?

She drove past the building whose address she had been given. It looked as if it had once been a motel. Was Jack inside? From a public booth she called the operator and asked for the telephone number of Jack Parry, giving the address.

"That's an unlisted number, ma'am."

"But this is an emergency. I have to get in touch with him."

"I'm sorry. I cannot give out that information. Perhaps if you called the police."

"Thanks."

"Should I put you through?"

Louise hung up. She drove aimlessly, telling herself that she was not meant to get in touch with Jack. God was putting obstacles in her way and she should be glad. What sort of foolishness would she get involved in if she just went down to the truckstop and there was Jack? By the time she got home she was half convinced she was glad she had missed Jack.

His car was parked at the curb next door. Louise kept on going to the corner, turned, parked, waited. She breathed very shallowly, keeping her mind clear. If not finding Jack had been providential, running into him like this seemed to put a divine sanction on her intention to follow him when he left.

That is what she would do. Wait here until he drove off and then follow him wherever he went. She did not begin to think what lay at the end of the route. After five minutes, it occurred to her that Jack had come to see Tommy. He had the right to see his son once a week although he didn't always come.

But when Jack drove by twenty minutes later he was alone. Once in pursuit of him, she realized what anyone would think of what she was doing. Ellen, for example. She didn't care what Willis thought. What would Jack think, that was the important thing? Following his car, seeing him behind the wheel, wondering if he would notice her in his rearview mirror, she recalled their meeting at the truckstop and now the memory seemed ambiguous. Had he made fun of her or what? No matter how she turned her memories, she found it difficult to imagine that he had been interested in her. She was just another woman to him.

Well, that's all she wanted to be. She didn't want to marry him, for heaven's sake. She tossed her head, seeking the mannerism that would express her devil-may-care attitude.

It became clear that Jack was heading for the river. Louise felt a sinking sensation. He had come to see Tommy, the boy had not been home, and now he was going to look for him in a likely spot.

When he turned in the access road, Louise drove on for fifty yards then pulled over to the side of the county road and turned off her engine. She got out of the car and eased the door shut as if Jack might hear if she slammed it. She went rapidly across the field toward the woods and only felt safe when she entered them. She leaned against a sycamore, its smooth barkless trunk cool on her hand. Looking up through its branches to the blue sky beyond she seemed to be up there looking down, seeing this ridiculous middle-aged woman in pursuit of a man for whom she had no respect at all. Jack had been awful to Ellen and Ellen was her friend.

She heard the sound of someone approaching and stepped behind the tree, holding her breath. The footsteps stopped and then she heard another sound. She looked out from behind the tree and saw Jack pushing dirt away from something. He pulled the plastic bag free and held it up. It was the skull! Louise covered her mouth and withdrew behind the tree. After a moment there was the sound of Jack going away. She waited where she was, watched him go toward the road and his car. My God, he would notice hers. But he opened the trunk of his car, put the plastic bag inside and drove away.

Louise went to where Jack had unearthed the plastic bag with the skull in it. She looked around, shivering, wondering if there were other grisly trophies to be found here.

She began to dig around with the toe of her shoe.

NINETEEN

When Bonnie came out of the bathroom, Jack was already in bed, lying on his back, arms folded behind his head, eyes closed. She pulled back the covers and slipped in beside him.

Her toes touched something and she pushed at it, then withdrew her foot quickly. Jack was breathing regularly, his eyes still closed. Bonnie sat on the edge of the bed, lifted the covers, and saw the plastic bag.

She grabbed it and was holding it before she realized that it was looking at her. Large empty eyes, a grinning smile.

She screamed, stumbling away from the bed, and lost her balance. She fell with a great crash against the bathroom door. Jack bounded out of bed and knelt beside her.

"You all right?"

He was worried, the sonofabitch, she might have been seriously hurt. Her tailbone felt as if she had cracked it, but she didn't think so.

"What in God's name was that?"

"The skull?"

His face was close to hers, brows lifted, his eyes widened, innocent, concerned.

"Skull!"

"Probably one of your ancestors."

She had steadied herself against the wall and when she began to bang him on the chest with the heels of her hands she got a lot of leverage into it. He grabbed her wrists but she got one free and dug into his face with her nails.

"Jeez!" He bounded away from her and blood appeared on his cheek. His eyes blazed with anger and Bonnie readied herself for what she feared would be her punishment. She cowered when he came for her but he stepped over her and went into the bathroom, pushing his face close to the mirror. "You got any alcohol?"

"Bourbon or scotch?"

He grinned. It was over. She looked at the plastic bag lying on the bed. It caught and reflected light and she couldn't make out now what was in it. But she had seen all she wanted of that ghastly thing. She went into the bathroom and lay her face against his back.

"Get it out of here, Jack."

"I thought two heads would be better than one."

"Please."

He turned and took her in his arms. The feel of his hard body against her, not a spare pound on him, you'd think he worked out at the Y or ran ten miles every day, but as far as Bonnie knew he never exercised. Maybe sex cut his appetite. Or drugs.

She had watched him take the stuff, turned away but saw him in the dresser mirror, pouring it out and inhaling it. Selfish. Not that she would have joined him if he asked. She was into enough stupid things as it was. Now there was talk of the stuff being available on playgrounds so she no longer wondered how Jack got hold of it in a town the size of Wyler.

Once when they were sitting in a booth after their shift, Phyllis put on a knowing look and suggested that the truckstop was where it came in. With her snood off, Phyllis looked like an old maid schoolteacher. She cupped one elbow in her hand, and held her cigarette in two extended fingers, hoity-toity.

"Someone offer you something?"

Phyllis let her lids go to half-mast. "Maybe I'm wrong." She said it like maybe water isn't wet.

Bonnie kept her eyes open after that, but she never noticed anything. Not at the truckstop. If it did come in there, that would explain why Jack always had it. If he wasn't on the stuff, she might have asked him about Phyllis's theory.

Today had been different.

"One of Jack's girls was looking for him," Phyllis chirped.

"Uhhuh." Phyllis was jealous and not to be trusted on the matter of Jack Parry.

"The one who was here before."

Bonnie shrugged and made a tour of her station, giving coffee refills. She didn't want Phyllis to see her reaction.

Louise Long, that's who Phyllis meant, though she wouldn't know the woman's name. That bitch had been the cause of a real argument betwen her and Jack. Maybe Bonnie couldn't stop him from catting around but she was damned if she was going to have him meeting other women right under her nose at the Indy Truckstop. She was sure he would give her the kiss-off, although that would have been better than letting him make a fool of her in front of Phyllis. But Jack nodded and agreed that it was a reasonable request. He showed her a palm, rolled out his lower lip.

"You got it."

"All right."

His quick agreement deflated her. She had been ready for fireworks. That didn't mean she was the only woman in his life, of course, she wasn't a dreamer. Even if he was divorced, there was his wife. Bonnie had seen the house in Bel Air, a nice place. She had seen his wife and kid and couldn't for the life of her understand why he had left all that for the life he led now. She was drawn back to the suburban house again and again and that is how she found out that it was the woman next door who had come to see him at the truckstop. That was the woman who'd come looking for him today.

Bonnie's angry hatred of Louise Long seemed as much a defense of Jack's discarded wife as of her own interest.

TWENTY

Yesterday Jerome Blatz had taken the pickup out to the Indy Truckstop to have new brake linings installed. The mechanics there were the best in the area, the cost was less than it would have been at the dealer he had bought the pickup from, and he could pass the time waiting in the dining room where the coffee had real body, not the watery brew you got most everywhere nowadays. He found he could think better in a busy place.

All his life he had spent whole days alone, riding machinery over the land, working around the place, solitary, by himself. Oh, Maud was always in the house, usually in the kitchen, the goddam radio going from the crack of dawn until she went yawning upstairs at seven-thirty. A good woman but no one you could have much of a conversation with. That isn't why he'd married her, though, so he wasn't complaining. She was a warm affectionate woman when she wasn't dead tired. No, he had no complaints about Maud.

The fact was he preferred to think things through on his own, but in order to do that he had to be distracted. God only knew how much time he'd wasted at the mall, sitting on a bench, the fountain splashing behind him, the restful distraction of the flow of shoppers endlessly passing. The buzz in his head stopped, his mind cleared, and life lay before him like a clean empty road.

Sitting at the counter in the dining room of the truck-stop had the same effect. The buxom waitress kept up a chatter as she moved around behind the counter, pouring refills, talking back to the cook when she went to the window for orders, forever swiping away at the counter with a wet rag—and Jerome found it conducive to meditation.

If the season were right, he could have taken the tractor out. Going back and forth across a field, straight row after straight row, lulled him into thinking, but Maud would think he'd lost his mind if he got out the tractor today. So there he was at the truckstop ready to think it through.

There were times when he regretted playing it cute and going to Andrew Broom with the offer Frank McGough had made for his riverside property. At the time he hadn't been tempted by the money, but it was an excuse to visit Andrew, if only to be talked out of selling. But he found out that his land wasn't the only plot being bid for, with Bink Philips sitting in the outer office waiting to talk to Andrew. And now he had entered into a coalition with Bink and Wendell Jensen and if there was any way he could get out of it without losing the sale he'd do it. Only there wasn't any way he could drop his partners without getting Andrew mad at him.

So his problem came down to this: Should he stick with Andrew and take what he could get as part of a coalition, or should he switch to Frank McGough and close the deal? He was pretty sure he'd do better that way—on the sale of his land, but what would the implications be of dropping Andrew? No use kidding himself, if he dropped out of the coalition he stopped being Andrew Broom's client.

"I'm waiting for my pickup," Jerome told the waitress when she offered him a fourth refill.

"I hope you mean your truck."

"My pickup truck." Jerome stared at the grinning waitress, wondering what she meant.

"Forget it."

"This is the best garage in town. I bring my truck out here because the mechanics are better, they do the work right away and it's cheaper."

"So you're from Wyler."

Jerome was surprised, but of course she would think a truckstop customer was just passing through, a stranger. He half wished he hadn't explained his presence here. Her name was Bonnie according to the plastic tag.

"Outside of Wyler. I own a farm."

She shifted her weight and an odd expression flicked across her face. "I was raised on a farm. When I was a kid, I hated it, the work. Right now I'd give anything to be back on a farm."

"It's still a lot of work." This woman would never last on a farm, she was restless, probably had been all her life, itching to be somewhere else. Not at all like Maud. A woman had to be sure of herself, content way deep down inside, in order to live as much alone as a farm wife did.

"This place is no picnic."

Maybe not, but Bonnie seemed to enjoy it. She perked up when the mechanic came in and told Jerome his pickup was ready.

"That thing runs like a watch. You ever want to sell it, let me know," he added.

"I believe in taking care of machinery."

"Not everyone does, Mr. Blatz."

Jerome was surprised the mechanic knew his name, but of course he would have found it in the truck. His name was Jack Parry. Funny place, the truckstop, everyone wore a name tag telling you who they were. He felt anonymous without one.

That was yesterday. He needed another day of thinking about the land sale, but now his mind was made up. He used the upstairs phone, out of range of Maud, and telephoned Frank McGough's office. Keeping his voice down, hunched over the phone, he told the lawyer that he would like to talk. Confidentially.

"I can see you immediately, Jerome."

"I can't come there."

He told McGough that he would meet him at the parcel McGough's client wanted to buy. He couldn't risk being seen going into McGough's office. Contacting the lawyer was a kind of betrayal, at least people might think of it that way, but Jerome had made up his mind. He meant to get the best deal for his land possible and he didn't need Andrew Broom for that.

There was a car parked on the country road when he reached the public access to the river and at first Jerome thought McGough had beaten him there but the only way the lawyer could have done that was if he'd spoken from a car phone and that hadn't been the case, he'd called him. Jerome had half a mind to drive on by and stand McGough up. It had been his idea but now he thought their meeting was more likely to be witnessed out in the open than downtown. But what the hell, now that he was here he was here. He turned the pickup into the access road and drove slowly toward the river. It had always irked him a bit, this public access slam bang next to his property. Anyone from town had as much right to the river as he did, but of course mainly it was kids come to fish, and it was hard to resent that.

The road turned sandy and Jerome brought the pickup to a halt, turned off the motor and got out. From where he stood, he could see the car parked further on up the county road. Whoever it was hadn't approached the river on this road if he could read its surface and he thought he could. His own shoes had sunk inches into the soft sand when he got out of the truck. Walking on that road was like wading and anyone would have left a trail. The owner of the car could have crossed the open field and gone through the stand of trees to the river. Jerome drifted in the direction of the woods.

In among the trees, he felt invisible, but he moved on in the expectation of meeting someone, the owner of that parked car. At the back of his mind was the unexpressed thought that he might come upon some lovers doing it in the woods. So his eyes and ears were sharp as he moved along. Even so he damned near tripped over the woman.

He danced back from the body, crying out loud, "Excuse me, I'm sorry, I didn't see you."

But then he saw that the woman would never move again. The back of her head was a bloody mess and her open mouth pressed against the earth. The eye he could see seemed to be staring very intently at nothing.

God in heaven, she was dead. Killed.

The thought made his whole body tingle. He looked around, but the trees did not enable him to see far. The thought that someone might find him there sent him scampering back to his pickup. He burst out of the woods to find a young man standing by the pickup truck. Jerome came to a stop.

"Who're you?"

"Mr. Blatz?"

"I don't know you."

"My name is Lindel. James Lindel. From Frank McGough's office. He sent me here to meet you."

Jerome almost told the young fellow he didn't know what he was talking about. McGough knew they'd spoken on the phone but if Jerome did nothing further the lawyer would just forget it. Like hell. Jerome had suggested they meet here and sooner or later that woman's body was going to be found.

"Good. See that car parked out on the county road."

Lindel turned, then nodded. Hadn't he noticed it before?

Jerome said, "I got here a few minutes ago, saw that car, figured she couldn't have walked in on this road . . ."

"She?"

"I found her in the woods just before you got here."

"Found her?"

"She's dead."

Lindel actually took a step backward. "Is that why you wanted to meet here?"

"Hell no! I didn't know she was there. Come on and take a look."

"There's a dead woman in those woods?"

"That's right."

"Then I think we better call the sheriff."

"You better take a look at her first."

But the young man shook his head. "I'll take your word for it."

Lindel had parked behind Jerome and he had a car phone. Jerome's mind was racing as he followed the young man to the car.

"I'll talk to the sheriff," he said. "I found the body."

But Lindel put through the call and Jerome stood there listening to the young lawyer tell Earl Waffle who he was, where he was calling from, and that he was acting as an officer of the court. "I have a man here says there's a dead woman in the woods near the river." A pause. "No. I thought you should do that, Sheriff."

"Tell him who I am, goddam it."

But Lindel had cut the connection.

"Can I use that thing?"

"Who you want to call?"

"My lawyer. Andrew Broom."

Jerome did not like the way the young man smiled when he handed him the cellular phone.

TWENTY-ONE

"Jerome Blatz has been arrested," Susannah said after entering his office and shutting the door. Andrew Broom did not look up.

"Speeding?"

"Suspicion of murder."

Susannah seemed serious. Andrew waited for more.

"He could hardly speak when he called. Hyperventilating. Then he began to cry."

"Jerome?"

"I told him you'd be right over."

"Where's Gerald?"

"Golfing."

"Lucky him."

At the courthouse, Andrew asked to see his client. Jerome looked into the visiting room and, when he saw Andrew, came scooting across the room toward him. "Get me out of here!"

"Sit down, Jerome. I want to hear the story from you."

Waffle had explained the situation with undisguised relish. Jerome Blatz, the world-class sonofabitch, was in his jail on a legitimate charge. Waffle's manner suggested that he did not really believe that Jerome was responsible for the death of the woman whose body had been found in the woods just to the east of the public access road to the Tippecanoe. Andrew was disposed to enjoy the situation himself until he heard that it was Lindel who had called the police.

"What was he doing there?"

"He said he was keeping an appointment with Blatz."

That Jerome had arranged to meet the nephew of Frank McGough put a very different light on events. Thus far Jerome's story had made no allusion to Lindel.

"You telephoned the sheriff when you found the body?"

"I don't have a phone in the truck, Andrew."

"Where did you call from?"

"Andrew, I didn't do it. You don't think I'd kill someone, do you? A woman? I don't even know who she is."

"Her name is Louise Long."

"Never heard of her."

"What were you doing down by the river, Jerome?"

"Is going down to the river against the law? I own land there, as you well know."

"A man named Lindel called the sheriff."

"He the guy with the car phone?"

"He's a lawyer. He's the nephew of Frank McGough."

A minor moral drama played across the creased face of Jerome Blatz. If there were some lie he could tell that would deflect Andrew's attention from the presence of Lindel he would have told it; the truth was a painful thing. Tears stood in Jerome's eyes and began to leak down his face.

"I was about to do a bad thing, Andrew."

"With the woman?"

"Not with the woman, goddam it! Andrew, you know my character. You know I couldn't . . ."

"Deceive? Betray? Sell out?"

Jerome put his face in his hands and his shoulders shook.

Andrew had every right to refuse to represent Jerome Blatz and he found the prospect of leaving the now chastened farmer to his fate tempting. Unfortunately, if he did, Jerome's fate would very likely include Frank McGough. And it was his attempt to deal with Frank that had gotten Jerome into this mess.

"Why were you meeting someone from McGough's office on the banks of the Tippecanoe, for crying out loud?"

"Andrew, let me just say it right out. I intended to go back on my word. You know and I know that I sat in your office and agreed to act together with Bink and Wendell. Well, I wanted to take a look at the possibility of a private deal." Jerome sat straighter and moved forward on his chair. "A sensible business deal. That's what I was looking into."

"You're a little late, Jerome."

"How so?"

"Wendell already sold his parcel and Bink Philips is about to do the same."

"Because of what I've done?"

"They beat you to the punch, Jerome. You're no worse than they are. And no better. All three of you made a damned fool out of me."

"They backed out of our deal!" Apparently sincere indignation shone in Jerome's eyes as he lifted off his chair.

"Settle down, Jerome, or they'll take you back to your cell."

With this reminder of his plight gloom settled over

Jerome Blatz. His mouth trembled but he did not cry. His face looked like the tragic mask over the stage in the auditorium of Tarkington High.

"Being undercut by your supposed partners is the least of your troubles. I'll ask my question again. I know what you were meeting about; I want to know why you were meeting where you were."

"Secrecy."

"Whose idea was that?"

"Mine."

"You suggested meeting there?"

"Andrew, I told him I couldn't risk being seen going into his office. Maybe if I had, I'd have run into Bink and Wendell." Jerome made a disgusted sound. "Why didn't McGough tell me he already had Wendell's land?"

"Let's stick to the point, Jerome. You said you didn't want to meet in his office. I'll ask again. Who suggested meeting where you did?"

Jerome screwed up his face as he thought. Some intimation of the point of the question made him see the importance of his answer. There was a moment when Jerome's darting eyes suggested a lie was about to be told. But then Jerome looked away. "I did."

"Why not at your farm?"

"Maud."

Maud probably was kept out of the details of most of Jerome's dealings in the division of labor their marriage represented. But it said much about Jerome's notion of what he was doing that he didn't want Maud as a witness. The hope that Jerome had been lured to that particular spot to make a grisly discovery dissolved. Probably just as well. Finding the body had been just a coincidence, that was Jerome's story, and it was on that basis that Andrew meant to tell the judge that it was ludicrous to hold Jerome Blatz.

TWENTY-TWO

Pascal Pence, reporter for the *Wyler Dealer*, was always on the alert for female role models, women she could respect, look up to, emulate, and Phillipa seemed to fill the bill from the first time Pascal interviewed the wife of Clark Cooper. The limpid eyes abrim with disappointment in the world, the sun-streaked honey-colored hair drawn into a loose thick plait that hung down her back and seemed to pull her head back and tilt her chin upward, could have provided a model for a statue of Justice. Had that wide mouth ever worn lipstick? There were tiny creases at the corners of her eyes.

"How long have you lived in Wyler?"

"Ever since I met Clark."

"I came here right out of the university," Pascal said, doubtful the older woman cared. "A year ago."

"How do you like it?"

"It's a start."

The mouth widened in a gentle smile. "A stepping-stone."

"Yes."

"To what?"

Pascal waved her hand. The answer seemed self-evident. She had not spent those years in school to live out her life on the *Wyler Dealer*.

"This is what I had been searching for," the older woman said.

Phillipa gave her a sketch of the trajectory that had brought her here, the more or less wife of Clark Cooper, champion of the rights of Native Americans. "Cities are larger, there are more people, but they are dangerous now. Be glad you're here in a community where you can become known and come to know a significant number of your fellow citizens."

But nothing ever happened in Wyler. Phillipa was as bad as Humphrey Ward. Maybe both were simply making the best of a bad deal, one they realized was permanent. Maybe Phillipa wasn't a role model after all. She insisted on submerging her life in that of Clark Cooper.

"Why did you marry him?"

"For the sake of the tribal ceremony." She looked serenely at Pascal, inviting misunderstanding, disapproval, curiosity.

Pascal had come to interview Phillipa about Boyd Carlson's anti-gambling crusade but could not get the woman off the subject of Indians. Did she really think that the whole point of the campaign was to make life more difficult for Clark Cooper and his ragtag band of followers?

"It's part of a pattern. Now they're desecrating our burial grounds."

"I don't understand."

"It's been in your paper."

She meant the death of Louise Long. Pascal had covered that story, arriving after the body was discovered. Jerome Blatz was at first wary, darting away from her, then determined to give her his side of the story although he did not like this description of what he had to say.

"It's not a story and it's not my side. It's what happened. I noticed the car, saw no signs that anyone had been walking in the road, figured the driver must have gone over in those woods and went to take a look."

Lean slack-jawed face, bulging eyes, Pascal would bet he suspected a couple had disappeared into the woods and had gone to spy on them. And found a body. Lindel? He said he had come in response to Jerome Blatz's request for a meeting.

"At the river?"

Blatz looked as if he would like to deny he had made an appointment with the lawyer. He said he'd had a question, a technical question, one he didn't want to put to his own lawyer. "I have a lawyer. Andrew Broom."

His voice dropped as he said it and he turned away from Lindel. Pascal's eye was drawn to where the coroner and his assistant were tending to the body. She was reminded of the medical examiner's crew with which she had spent a summer in Indianapolis, at first appalled by the grisly trade, eventually admiring their work. By contrast, the county coroner looked amateurish.

Now in the interview, Phillipa drew the connection between the skull and Indian burial grounds and desecrating graves but that meant that if anyone had a grievance it was the people Phillipa spoke for rather than Jerome Blatz. There had been signs of digging where Louise was found, but no bones, no indication at all that the place had once been a burial ground. But even if it weren't, even if it was only thought to be, that could have motivated one of Phillipa's Native Americans to avenge himself—or herself—on the desecrating white man.

"Have you ever been at that spot near the river?"

"I have visited all the local sites that involve the history of my people."

"Lately?"

Phillipa shrugged off the question. "We shall be keeping a vigil there throughout the night. The television station is sending a crew."

The local television station had once been the property of the Wards but Humphrey's mother sold it off in disgust when she saw what news became on the tube. She had been certain the medium could not last. It had been a major mistake.

"Financially," Humphrey emphasized. "She was absolutely right about television news."

There was a point of time somewhere between Humphrey's childhood and her own that divided people into two groups, those who could imagine the world without television and those who could not. Pascal of course fell into the second class. She could understand how this or that on television could be criticized, but the whole medium? It was crazy. The competititon between the paper and WYCB was constant and unequal. If it really was a. competition. Some people settled for TV alone, the rest needed the paper too. Pascal figured you could count the people in Wyler who did not watch television.

"Will your paper cover the vigil?"

"I go where I'm sent."

"The motto of a free press."

"I don't own the paper."

"I've never understood how anyone could own a newspaper." Phillipa spoke with the pained deliberation of a child. What was the alternative? Phillipa might be a woman of striking good looks but Pascal decided she was naive.

Humphrey listened to her conjecture that one of Phillipa's people had as good a reason as anyone else to kill Louise Long.

"Waffle says it might have been her husband."

"Why?"

"They didn't get along."

"Did he drive her to the river?"

"Ask Waffle. It's his idea."

If the coroner seemed amateurish to Pascal, the sheriff verged on the comic. He had reason to think Louise and Willis hadn't gotten along but no evidence at all that the husband had been down by the river at the time his wife was killed. Pascal talked to Ellen Parry, Waffle's major source on the Long marriage. Pascal had interviewed Mrs. Parry before, when she had talked with people at the middle school about drugs. She found a woman distraught that anything she had said about her neighbors might give rise to the suspicion that Willis had killed Louise.

"Have you talked with him?"

"Not yet."

"He couldn't hurt a fly. Louise used to say he couldn't move fast enough to catch a fly. Besides, I don't know if he was as bored with her as she was with him."

"Bored."

"Louise always thought other people had more exciting lives than she did." Ellen glanced toward the house next door. "She had everything most women want and yet she was unhappy."

"Were you friends, you and Louise?"

A tearful nod. "Yes. Oh what in the world was she doing down there by the river all by herself?"

"She wasn't by herself."

"Why do you say that?"

"The one who killed her was there too."

Pascal was patient while the woman cried. After a minute, she offered her a Kleenex.

"Did your husbands get along?"

This had the effect of prolonging the crying. It turned out that Mrs. Parry was divorced.

Pascal was surprised to find that Phillipa knew Jack Parry.

"He goes with my sister-in-law. More or less. He's a chaser."

The opinion was widespread. Pascal had lunch at the Indy Truckstop, not quite knowing why. Identifying Bonnie, Phillipa's sister-in-law, was no problem. A woman just trembling on the edge of middle age, ready to go gray and fat, slow of foot behind the counter, yet clearly enjoying life. Pascal sat in another station and watched her. It was difficult to know why any man would prefer her to Ellen. Not that she didn't look like fun. A lot more fun than Phillipa. But Ellen was pretty, beautiful even, womanly . . . Ellen Parry was everything Pascal had no intention of becoming but she assumed that was the kind of woman a man preferred.

Of course it was Ellen's viewpoint that counted in the stories Pascal had been writing about the sudden appearance of drugs near Wyler schools. Ellen Parry had spoken with the shock of a parent as well as a school employee when she checked out the chatter of kids going through the food line and realized it was true. Drugs were being sold, there were dealers among the kids. Ellen was angry and felt it should be simple to shut it down, punish the offenders, make the schools safe. Pascal felt like an apologist for corruption when she explained the legal difficulties. Of course the main problem was Waffle and his deputies. One major difficulty was enough for them to handle and the death of Louise Long had taken over center stage at the sheriff's office.

"I know Phillipa," Pascal said, when she switched to Bonnie's counter and ordered coffee.

"Phillipa."

"Your sister-in-law."

Bonnie waited. Knowing Phillipa was obviously no recommendation with her. Pascal told Bonnie she was with the paper, that she was working on the death of Louise. It was neither the time nor place to have a conversation with Bonnie, not that the waitress looked all that eager to have one anyway. A very good-looking man came in and Bonnie swarmed all over him. Jack Parry? The man became aware of her staring and his eyes sparked when they met hers. Bonnie turned to see who he was looking at, then moved to block his line of vision. Her duties took her away again and again and whenever they did Pascal was aware of Jack Parry's eyes on her. Phillipa had called him a chaser. Pascal believed it.

He stopped at her side on his way out. "You the reporter?"

She told him who she was, professionally extending her hand, trying to ignore his unnervingly good looks.

"You in sports or what?" A grin.

"I cover everything."

"Everything," he repeated, no modulation in his voice, but somehow it was suggestive anyway. Bonnie came back, glowering, and Jack Parry left.

"She was after Jack Parry," Phillipa said when Pascal talked to her of the murder at riverside. "The woman who was killed."

"How do you know that?"

"Bonnie was furious."

Pascal did not pursue it. It seemed like just a diversion, another trail for her to pursue. A Jack Parry saddled with a discontented housewife, nagged by Bonnie, might have wanted to rid himself of his burden.

Pascal hated herself for engaging in such fancies. It was the antithesis of reporting. Playing guessing games was a waste, if only because she couldn't write up guesses and turn them in. Two nights after she first saw Jack Parry at the truckstop he telephoned. She said she remembered him.

"I wondered if you're free tonight."

"Free?"

"I thought we could have a few drinks, some laughs."

"I've met your wife."

A pause. "She divorced me. It was the worst thing that ever happened to me in my whole life."

Pascal felt her heart turn over at his words. His voice was not the voice of a lady-killer but of a man whose life had fallen apart. When he repeated his suggestion that they get together, the basis seemed changed. He needed someone to talk with.

TWENTY-THREE

Bonnie told herself the reporter was a professional woman, doing a job, a good-looking girl who would see Jack Parry as a middle-aged man, a comic rather than attractive figure. Uh huh. Once the reporter was aware of Jack's interest, she perked up visibly. Bonnie recognized the signs with a sinking heart. Why did she put up with the bastard?

Because after a fling he came back to her, the way he used to go back to his wife. Well, not quite. To hear Jack tell of her, Ellen Parry was a plaster saint.

"Was she any good in bed?"

Bonnie thought he was going to hit her when she asked the question. Jack was a funny guy, no doubt about it. He couldn't get enough yet the suggestion that he and his wife had slept together was an insult. She gave up.

Only she didn't give up, agonizing whenever his eye roamed, never sure until it was over that he would come back to her. The smart thing would be to get over him, let the thing die, learn to live alone and like it. At her age, that shouldn't be difficult, life would be a lot more peaceful. Sometimes she thought she clung to Jack just to prove something to Phyllis and Clark and Phillipa.

"A skull!" Phillipa cried, when Bonnie told her about the stunt Jack had pulled.

"I felt something when I got into bed and that's what it was." Bonnie shuddered at the memory but she couldn't help smiling. And of course it was nice letting Phillipa in on how much fun she and Jack had together.

"Where did he get it?"

"I don't know."

"Where is it now?"

"Do you want it, for God's sake?"

"Yes! Bonnie, that must be the skull that was written of in the paper. I've tried to find out more about it but the paper claims it was all anonymous."

Bonnie didn't know what she was talking about. Some woman calling in to the paper and claiming a neighbor kid had a human skull in his room. Phillipa was sure that skull had come from one of the burial grounds Native Americans had used in the area.

"Where did Jack get it?"

"I don't know."

"Doesn't he have a son?"

"Look, you want the thing, you can have it."

Phillipa wanted it badly enough to drive her home right then and there to get it. Bonnie felt a little ghoulish, getting the thing out from the back of her closet, from under the pile of dirty clothes she tossed into a corner. She wrapped it in paper towels and took it out to Phillipa's car.

"Put it in back."

Phillipa wouldn't touch it. It wasn't that she was scared, it was because it was something sacred. That

113

was the first time she spoke of reburial. Bonnie went back to the mobile home with Phillipa.

It had seemed the thing to do, letting Phillipa have the damned thing, but nothing she did was right anymore. There was no way Phillipa would ever have let up on her if she hadn't turned over the skull to her. Maybe if Jack hadn't been chasing after the reporter, Bonnie would have held firm, let him decide, but she was on her own, Phillipa was relentless, she turned it over. Jack was mad as hell.

"It wasn't yours!"

"Oh wasn't it? I found it in my bed, didn't I?"

"My son found that, Bonnie. I took it to keep him out of trouble. The kid . . . well, you'd have to know him. It's the sort of thing he finds and keeps."

Sure, his son the genius, she had heard all about the kid. Jack wouldn't talk much about his wife but you couldn't shut him up about the kid. She was glad to have the yucky thing out of her apartment, out of her closet, gone. Let Phillipa make a big deal out of it if she wanted.

And anyway Bonnie was uneasy. When she read about the woman found dead near the river, it was just a name, an address, and neither had connected for her but then reading the obituaries she came upon the little postage stamp of a picture and she realized this was the dame who had come pestering Jack at the truckstop, the neighbor lady. God knows what Jack had been up to with her in the past. And now she was dead.

A dreadful thought came to her but Bonnie drove it from her mind. Dumb. Ridiculous. As ridiculous as Phyllis's stupid remark that Jack had something going over in the garage. If there had been a female mechanic over there, that would have been something else. But then Phyllis said what she meant and Bonnie gripped her arm.

"That's a lie."

Phyllis was feeling pain, but pleasure too because she knew she had rattled Bonnie. Phyllis was now going with a skinny guy whose throat rose out of his work shirt like a stalk, a great Adam's apple riding up and down in it. Felix. It was Felix who had told Phyllis that once a week a truck rolled in from Chicago and nobody, absolutely nobody but Jack Parry worked on it.

"So what? Felix hasn't been here long enough to realize that Jack Parry attracts business from all over the country. There are dozens wouldn't let anyone else work on their rigs but Jack."

"But there's never anything wrong with these trucks. That's Felix's point."

"A little advice, to you and Felix. Don't start anything. I don't think Jack would take kindly to that kind of rumor."

Jack Parry as messenger boy, that was the suggestion. Something came in on those trucks and something went out and only Jack worked on them. Of course Bonnie believed it. She'd wondered why he settled for work in a garage. He was good at it, better than most, but he could have done other things, better things. Bonnie had an idea how much Jack made as a mechanic and she realized that somehow she'd already known that wasn't the whole story on his income. Once when he was short they stopped at a bank. She figured he'd use the drive-through window but he parked and went inside. Bonnie stayed in the car but she could see him sign a slip and go through a gate and into the vault behind the counter. He was out again in five minutes. Later, she checked what he'd put into his shirt pocket when he came out of the vault. A key. He had several others like it, different, but like it. Safe deposit boxes. Whatever stash Jack had was in cash.

What Felix told Phyllis fit in with what Bonnie knew

115

of Jack's habit. Snorting junk like that, he should have been broke, but it was just the opposite. It made sense that he was in on the delivery rather than the receiving end. She had even tried to tell herself that the neighbor woman was a customer making a pest of herself, not another one of his girls.

"Get it back." He meant the skull and he meant she should get it back.

"No. You want it, you get it."

"You gave it to Clark?"

"Phillipa."

His expression changed. He might have said it aloud. Hell, I can handle Phillipa. As far as Bonnie knew he had never had any luck with her—of course he came on strong with her, but he came on strong with everyone— but she didn't mean to give him the opportunity. If he ever made out with Phillipa or Phyllis she'd kill him. It was humiliating enough when she didn't even know who the other women were. She was lucky he hadn't tried to introduce one of his friends into her bed. You couldn't blame him for thinking she'd put up with any- thing. But balling Phillipa or Phyllis would have been worse than that. She'd kill him.

Before she had a chance to talk with Phillippa about the skull, the great hullabaloo about the sacred burial grounds went up. There would be a ceremony of rebur- ial and of purification because the burial grounds had been desecrated by the white man.

To Bonnie's relief, Jack took it for a joke. And he stopped bugging her about getting the skull back from Phillipa. A good thing. Bonnie had never figured out how she was supposed to get it. Please give me back my skull, I shouldn't have given it to you? Weird.

But weirder still was the thought that would not go away. Louise Long had been pestering Jack and she had ended up dead. One night Bonnie brought it up. It was

in the newspaper report that Louise had been killed by
a blow to the head, maybe by a shovel.

"They find a shovel on Blatz?"

If they had it wasn't in the paper. Blatz was the farmer
who had been arrested and was under suspicion for the
killing of Louise but Andrew Broom was his lawyer and
Bonnie took that as a sign Blatz was innocent.

"You mean he'll get off? You may be right. Broom
is good."

"Somebody killed her."

He stirred beside her. "It was Blatz."

"You sound like you know."

Lying in the dark beside her, his voice sounding bodi-
less, he told her of the way Louise had followed him
that day, when he had gone looking for his son Tommy.
He'd parked in the public access drive and when he
went looking for his son stumbled on the spot where
Tommy had reburied the skull. What the hell, he had
thought, let the kid have it. But first he'd have a little
fun with Bonnie. Anyway, after he recovered it, when he
was going back to the road, he noticed the other car. He
didn't let on but once behind the wheel, he studied it in
the mirror and recognized it as the Longs' sedan. It was
a car he'd worked on. And Louise was at the wheel.
What the hell was she doing here? The thought that she
had been following him came, of course. He drove off
but a mile away, made a U-turn and came back. Louise
was no longer in her car. There was a pickup parked off
the road, also empty. Well, well. Jack just kept on going.

"I recognized the pickup too. It belongs to Jerome
Blatz."

"You gonna tell the sheriff all this?"

"Oh sure."

"Why would he kill her?"

"A lovers' quarrel?" But Jack laughed as he said it.
"He probably hit her as a trespasser. The sonofabitch

117

couldn't stand the thought of anybody on his property. Ask hunters. He's salt and peppered more kids than McDonald's."

"But that's not his property."

"It's close."

"Maybe you should tell that reporter all this."

His hand moved toward her and then he was tickling her and she was thrashing around, trying to get away from him, laughing so hard there were tears in her eyes. Honest to God, he was nothing but a big kid.

TWENTY-FOUR

Belton had been at his lake place and feeling no pain when Andrew got hold of him and told the judge he was needed in court.

"First thing in the morning, Andrew, they're biting like flies." It was Belton's fiction that he was a dedicated angler and lived for the hours he could spend out on the lake pulling in fish. If Belton had a boat he'd never been seen in it. His fishing was done from the screened front porch of his cottage, Channel 9 bringing him the Cubs or Sox, a thermos of margaritas at his side, the history of one or another World War II battle in his lap. It seemed cruel to summon him back to Wyler.

"It's got to be today, Judge. The prosecutor wants to arraign Jerome Blatz and I want to arrange bail."

"Who?"

"Hacker." Didn't Belton remember the name of the county prosecutor?

"I meant the accused."

"Jerome Blatz. We can't have a citizen of his stature spending unnecessary time in jail."

"What did the sonofabitch do?"

"Nothing. Hacker will accuse him of Murder One."

"Sweet Jesus," Belton murmured and Andrew could imagine the judge licking his liquor-lubricated lips. Belton shared the general dislike of the wealthy local farmer who alternated between Cassandra-like laments about his financial condition and gloating over his success. Jerome seemed to think that if he could get you feeling sorry for him, you had to applaud his good luck. "What happens if I don't come in?"

"I'll insist we take him before Devoir."

"A justice of the peace!"

"I needn't remind you of the provisions for the swift execution of justice."

"But Devoir owes Blatz money. And they're related."

"It is now two-thirty. You can freshen up in ten, fifteen minutes, it's a twenty-minute drive in your condition. Let's say three."

"What do you mean my condition?"

"Just getting out from under the hot sun."

It was closer to three-thirty when Belton came out of his chambers, looked with distaste at the bench which represented a sinecure but which also seemed to remind him of chained oarsmen. His sister Mabel, his bailiff, sang out, "O yes, O yes," an imperfect memory from *Witness for the Prosecution*. Gene Hacker stretched the session out to an hour, unable to restrain himself now that he had Jerome Blatz at least momentarily in his power. Nonetheless, everything went as Andrew wished, as it must, and Jerome was free on bail.

"Fifty thousand dollars!" Jerome yelped when the amount was set. Judge Belton lowered his head and glowered at the defendant over the rims of his half glasses.

"Is that satisfactory, Counselor?"

"Yes, your honor," Andrew said.

"Is your client good for that amount?"

"We'll scrape it together somehow, your honor."

The court session served to provide a new object for Jerome's wrath. He had been cursing the sheriff and his deputies unrelentingly since his arrest. Now he could curse Belton too.

Over the next few days, Andrew learned a good deal about Louise Long, some via the newspaper, the rest thanks to Susannah's asking around. Willis Long revealed that his wife was the woman who had made the anonymous call to the paper about the boy who kept a human skull in his room. Andrew thought of the kid he had surprised in the woods there by the river.

Whatever all this might have led to, things were looking undeniably brighter for Jerome Blatz until they checked out the shovel in the back of his pickup.

Jerome called to say the sheriff had come with a warrant to look around his place but Andrew reassured Jerome. "It's all routine."

"It's all a bunch of BS."

"That's what I said."

And he meant it. Harassing Jerome took Waffle's mind off the mounting criticism in the letters to the editor of the *Dealer* demanding that something be done about the sale of drugs in and around Wyler schools. Making a nuisance of himself at the Blatz farm made the sheriff look on the job.

"He took my shovel."

That bothered Andrew and he called the sheriff to find that Jerome's shovel was already on its way to Indianapolis for examination by the Indiana Bureau of Investigation.

"Just routine, Andrew. The likely murder weapon was

a shovel. Jerome had a shovel in his pickup. Chances are this will get him off the hook once and for all."

"Just doing Jerome a favor, Earl?"

"You'll be the first to know the results."

Earl sounded flabbergasted when he called with the results. "I just got them by Fax, Andrew, and I'll be damned if they didn't find human hair and blood on Jerome's spade. They match the dead woman's. What do you make of that?"

Andrew had no immediate answer. "What made you send Jerome's shovel to the IBI?"

"I told you. The likely murder weapon was a spade. Jerome was on the spot in his pickup. I'm giving the truck the once-over, all legal, I had a warrant, and there is the damned spade."

"Jerome say it was his?"

"Now whose else's would it be?"

That was the question Andrew put to Jerome. He had gone out to the farm and they were sitting on opposite sides of the trestle table in the huge kitchen redolent of the day's baking. Maud's routine was pretty much what her mother's had been and two of the Blatz daughters were carrying on the same tradition now with their own families.

"Andrew, it'll be mine. You can bet on it. Whoever killed that woman took the spade from my truck and put it back afterward."

This was said without bombast, almost without expression, and Andrew had the overpowering sense that Jerome was right. But he also knew how weak an explanation this would seem, even to those of good will.

"So it must have been done on the spur of the moment."

"How so?"

"Someone deliberately setting out to kill the woman, would have brought the means to do it. He could not have counted on your showing up with a convenient weapon."

"He?" Maud asked over her shoulder. She stood at the stove, her back to the table, preparing another meal.

"Whoever."

"That spade could have been taken from the truck beforehand." Maud might have been speaking into the clouds of steam, addressing an oracle. But this was weaker still as an alternative. It did however have the advantage of suggesting that the deed had been done with forethought. And that in turn suggested it must have been someone who knew Louise. Someone with a motive. What possible motive could Jerome have had to bash in the head of a woman he did not even know?

"Andrew," Earl Waffle said, tipping back in his chair, "you know as well as I do that Blatz acted as if he owned all the land west of the river between county roads Q and R. To him that woman must have been a trespasser, and there she was, digging around in the woods. He lost it. He went to his truck, grabbed the shovel . . ."

The sheriff rose dramatically from his chair, snatched an imaginary spade and now advanced with menacing expression on the file cabinet in the corner of his office. He lifted his weapon, using both hands, and brought it viciously down.

"Adding her name to the dozens of other trespassers he has killed over the years."

Waffle looked steadily at Andrew. "He's all we got, Andrew. He owns the murder weapon. He was there. If I didn't charge him I would rightly be accused of delinquency."

"You are an officer of justice, Earl. I know you don't think Jerome did this."

"You don't know any such thing."

"Your job is to find out as much about that woman as

you can, her circle, her acquaintances, her enemies. Who had reason to want that woman dead?"

Earl was unconvinced but even more he was damned if he would take orders from Andrew Broom or any other defense attorney. He had the full weight of the IBI behind him now and he had no intention of dashing off in the direction Andrew suggested.

Which left it up to Andrew. Clearly the only way to defend Jerome Blatz was to produce the one, male or female, who had killed Louise Long.

TWENTY-FIVE

Bonnie carried the skull from the car and Phillipa took it gingerly with both hands, receiving it as a sacred object. She placed it on the drainboard beside the kitchen sink in the narrow mobile home and removed the wrappings.

"Jack will kill me for this," Bonnie said.

Phillipa ignored her. Bonnie clearly wanted to make what she had done the object of prolonged discussion so that she could savor the danger of acting contrary to the presumed wishes of Jack Parry.

"You did the right thing."

"I wish I was as sure as you are."

"Bonnie, for crying out loud. This was once the head of a human being. It sat on real shoulders. It was filled with brains and thoughts and felt as we do. And that person was an ancestor of yours. You know it's wrong to turn a person's skull into a toy or collectible."

But Phillipa argued with only half her mind, with the other half concentrating on the surprisingly small, discolored dome of bone sitting on the drainboard. The hole in the center of the forehead was the only blemish. Phillipa had no trouble imagining the white man's bullet coursing through that bony brow. The back of the skull bore the mark of the bullet's exit. She could imagine a young brave standing stoically in the parade ground of a rugged stockade, facing the firing squad with dignity and poise. The sound of the shot that killed him must have been the last thing he heard. Behind her, no longer heeded, Bonnie continued to ruminate on the significance of what she had done.

Later, after Bonnie was gone, Clark came into the trailer."What the hell is that?" Phillipa had waited for this, wanting to cherish his first reaction.

"The desecrated skull of your ancestor."

"Is it real?" Clark stayed where he was but leaned toward the skull. Phillipa had placed it on the mantel and its great hollow eyes registered the room like lenses.

"Yes."

"I don't want that goddam thing in my house."

Phillipa conquered her disappointment. "Of course you don't. It must be reinterred, put back in the earth from which it was criminally removed. There will be an enormous ceremony at which you will preside. We shall insist that representatives of state and local government take part. The city could be held accountable for this outrage and forced to pay significant compensation."

"Take it out of here."

"I've prepared a reliquary in the kitchen." A square cardboard box filled with weightless plastic peanuts.

Phillipa no longer found it odd that her own zeal exceeded Clark's but it was hard when he apparently did not see what a coup the recovery of this skull was. Protesting the banning of bingo as prejudicial had its limitations and a generic plea for just treatment of Native Americans ignited no fire of shame in the oppressive majority. But the desecration of Indian remains was very different indeed. The rhetorical possibilities in the narration of a boy's digging up and taking home and keeping as a trophy the skull of one of the people who had lived in freedom and dignity on this land long before the intrusion of the colonial oppressors—well, Phillipa thanked their tribal gods for this gift. Meanwhile she boxed up the skull and kept it out of Clark's sight. It helped to think that his distaste was prompted by the dreadful thing that had been done to his ancestor.

But if it was out of sight, it was not out of mind.

"Where'd you get it?" he asked from behind the raised kite of *Sporting News*.

"Bonnie."

The paper crumpled and he stared at her. "Where'd she get it?"

It was important to make the skull's itinerary seem both matter of fact and an incredible outrage. Jack Parry had put it under the covers of Bonnie's bed to give her a scare. Clark looked unblinkingly at her. She felt that any contempt he felt was directed at her rather than Bonnie's companion.

"It was Jack's son who brought the skull home. You remember the story in the paper. Without names, of course. The boy's mother made him return it, Jack retrieved it and brought it home to play his crude practical joke on Bonnie. She realized that it belonged with you."

"Me?"

By then, in her mind, Phillipa had planned and rehearsed the whole sequence of events. Step one would be to enlist the press. Whatever the attitude of the *Dealer* toward the plight of Native Americans, they could not resist a story like this. They had been unable to resist it when it was called into them anonymously.

"The reporter Pascal is on our side."

Phillipa was convinced of this. Ideologically, the young woman could not resist championing a people whose grievances were by now all but universally conceded. The desecration of their burial grounds gave it just the anti-religious note a secularized culture finds it irresistible to protest. The presumed reader could at once feel condescension toward those who thought bones were somehow sacred while at the same time piously championing their right to make fools of themselves.

"The media will be our vehicle for bringing the politicians to heel. The mayor, state senators and representatives, the governor, both senators . . ." Her voice trailed off as the vast procession formed before her mind's eye. Local television coverage would be picked up nationally, for a time at least the eye of the nation would be trained on Wyler, Indiana. How fitting that so dramatic a blow for Native Americans should take place in this misnamed state. The effects would radiate out and benefit all tribes and peoples.

Fantasy invited her to think of Clark as leader of a reinvigorated coalition of tribal leaders, demanding and at last achieving justice for his people. Seated across the room, the *Sporting News* hanging from one hand while with the other he lifted a can of beer to his mouth, Clark looked unfortunately like some reservation stereotype rather than a heroic figure. Could he be remade for this role? Did he have within him the wherewithal to rise to the occasion, seize the opportunity, and perform a legendary deed for his people? Alone, perhaps not. But she would be at his side.

"Where'd the kid find it?"

"By the river."

"Whereabouts by the river?"

The woods where the woman's body was found must be the site. It abutted on public land, a decided advantage, but the intrusion of Jerome Blatz into the drama provided another useful instrument for exciting a sense of public outrage. Blatz was engaged in negotiations to sell his adjacent property and would not have looked kindly on the reversion to Clark's people of what was now the public access to the Tippecanoe.

"What's the woman got to do with it?"

"That's the real ghoulish part."

He did not understand.

"Clark, she represented the first of possible hordes of souvenir hunters swarming over that ground, unearthing bones and artifacts."

He thought about that, then raised his paper. From behind it, he said, "I wish Bonnie had kept the damned thing."

"I know exactly how you feel."

TWENTY-SIX

Instinctively Humphrey agreed with Andrew Broom. It was preposterous to think that Jerome Blatz had taken a shovel and beaten the brains out of that woman found dead by the river. But that was feeling, loyalty, whatever. On the other hand was the undeniable fact that the IBI had found traces of the woman's blood and hair on Jerome's spade, the one he always carried in the pickup which he had driven to the murder scene. Andrew's suggestion that anyone could have taken the shovel and killed the woman and then returned it would never fly.

"Why return it, Andrew?"

"Good. That has to be pursued."

"I didn't suggest it was a lead."

"That's how the best ideas come, taking us unawares."

"The next time I'm accused of murder, I want you to represent me, Andrew."

"If you're as innocent as Jerome, I shall be delighted to."

130

"What if I'm as guilty as Jerome?"

"I said I'd be delighted. Jerome is innocent."

Straight-faced, unwavering voice, if Andrew did not mean what he was saying, Humphrey was a brain surgeon.

It was Andrew's contention that those who knew that Jerome could not possibly be guilty were duty bound to discover who had in fact done the deed.

"Who was Louise Long? What do we really know of this woman? One thing we do know. Among her acquaintances was one who wished her dead, someone who waited his time with great cunning, and when the opportunity presented itself acted with dispatch and cruelty. Returning the spade to Jerome's truck was masterful. We are looking for a resourceful person, someone shrewd, cold-blooded, and, in a way, desperate."

"You sound as if you had someone in mind."

"I have in mind whoever fits that description."

"Who was Louise Long?" Humphrey said in turn to Pascal Pence, steepling his fingers and squinting in the direction of his mother's portrait. "What do we really know of this woman? Pascal, I want to know who her friends and enemies were, how she spent her day. I want to know what she was doing roaming around in those woods at the time she was killed."

"They've pretty well nailed Jerome Blatz for the crime," Pascal said.

"The circumstantial evidence is admittedly strong. But it points to a pointless crime. I don't think it is fair to that woman to have it suggested that her life ended almost whimsically, because of an unmotivated, yet cruel, deed."

Through half-closed eyes he studied Pascal as he spoke. The tack he was taking did not seem to be effective.

"In any case, it is lazy journalism for us simply to

take the word of the sheriff and some experts in Indianapolis as to the guilt or innocence of one of our fellow citizens. If Jerome is the man, I say hang him from the highest tree. But if he isn't, I want to know that. I want to be able to say that the *Wyler Dealer* conducted its own investigation, explored every avenue, even the seemingly implausible."

"This is an assignment?"

"It is."

She saluted before standing, but then she hadn't meant to do him honor. As always, anger enhanced her loveliness. He looked up defiantly at his mother hanging on the wall. He was halfway through his forties. She could not claim that he was too soon made glad.

Louise Long's obituary conveyed something of the banality of her life, but as Pascal checked and verified the meager details, adding other equally boring ones as her inquiries continued, she was oppressed by the apparent pointlessness of the slain woman's life. The single interesting thing about her was that she had been killed with a shovel in a wood near the banks of the Tippecanoe River. She found herself composing a truer and more depressing version in her mind.

Born in Wyler, raised in Wyler, educated in Wyler, married to another native of Wyler with whom and their dreadful children she had lived in a suburb the design of whose houses seemed to be based on losing entries in an architectural contest—Gathering all this like evidence, Pascal felt more and more depressed. Her own tenure in Wyler seemed to threaten a life as dull and uninteresting as Louise's.

"She was not a happy woman," Ellen Parry said.

Pascal, ready for redeeming revelations, felt depression deepen when it became clear that it was the mysterious and exciting life of other Wylerites that had troubled Louise's imagination and made her restive in her suburban home.

"Why can't people be content with what they have?"

Pascal let a smile suffice for answer. Ellen herself seemed content, at least as much as her circumstances permitted.

"How long have you been divorced?"

Ellen remembered her wedding day, she remembered the birthday of her son, but she had blanked out the day when her marriage was dissolved. Pascal pursued the spoor of Ellen's life, if only as momentary relief from the sad tale of Louise Long.

"Were you both natives of Wyler?"

Yes. Pascal felt the walls of the house close in on her. They sat in a living room furnished with the kind of suites and lamps and tables featured in bleeding colors in Sunday supplements. On the wall hung framed silhouettes of ducks mounted on wood panels. There was an odd smell in the house.

"My son's chemistry set."

"How old is he?"

She listened to the enthralled account, even accepted when Ellen offered to show her Tommy's room. The dangling medical student's skeleton, the books, the chemistry lab, the computer, suggested something out of the ordinary Wyler way. Pascal feigned fright at the clacking skeleton.

"It's plastic. Not like the skull he brought home."

Skull? The memory did not form immediately but as Ellen went on it clicked. "We got a telephone call about that!"

Ellen made a little face. "Louise. Don't ask me why. I think she envied me Tommy."

Thinking of the bland progeny next door, Pascal could believe it.

"Where is it?"

"I made him take it back where he found it."

"Where was that?"

"I didn't want to know. By the river, I think."

Her eyes widened as she said it. She might have been thinking of the fact that Louise was found by the river.

"She didn't work?"

"Louise? She didn't have to."

"What she did do all day?"

"Well, she didn't take advantage of her situation. Keeping a house properly is a full-time job. Before my divorce, I didn't work and I seemed never to have a minute to myself. Of course, Louise's girls were in school and she had more freedom, but rather than use it she sat around being bored and wishing she was somewhere else."

If Louise had gone off on day trips to Chicago, done something genuinely interesting, Pascal could have found the beginnings of sympathy with the dead woman. Tommy came in as they were talking, rumpled, bashful, but beautiful. My God, what a good-looking man he would be. He mumbled and nodded and went on to his room. Ellen's pride was visible.

"He looks like you," Pascal lied.

"No, he's the image of Jack."

"Do you have any pictures of the two of you?"

In the wedding album, a very pretty Ellen stood beside the impossibly good-looking groom.

With an effort Pascal returned to Louise.

"What does Willis Long do?"

When she went next door to interview Willis she found him talking with Gerald Rowan.

TWENTY-SEVEN

Boyd Carlson's wife Wendy was the realtor equivalent of an ambulance chaser. She had inquired of Willis Long if he had any thought of selling the house. Not a bad ploy normally. The obituaries provided their own ghoulish leads, and Boyd had not been above a few posthumous inquiries himself. Willis's reaction was unprecedented. Apparently a mild man, Wendy's call released God knows how many years of pent-up fury. He exploded on the phone, he wrote an op ed article for the *Dealer*, he wired Boyd demanding to know what kind of a representative would prey on the grief of his constituents in the hope of a little profit. Blaming it on his wife would not have been a good idea. From his Indianapolis office, Boyd had Maxine put through a call to Willis.

She took the phone from her ear and looked at it. "He refused to hold. He said if you wanted to telephone him do it yourself, he wasn't going to sit around waiting for you to come on."

135

Ignore it? The counsel of cowardice was often pure wisdom and so it would have been in this case, as Boyd was ruefully to think in the days ahead. Perhaps if Maxine had not been sitting there wondering what the seasoned politician would do with an irate constituent, he would have settled for an obscene remark and turned to something else. Instead, he picked up the phone and as Maxine called out the numbers dialed.

"Willis Long."

"Mr. Long, this is Boyd Carlson calling. I want to apologize . . ."

"Oh no you don't."

"You won't accept an apology?"

"Not like this, not on the phone. Did you read my article in the *Dealer*?"

"I fully understand that you're upset and I do most sincerely . . ."

"Put it in writing. Send it to the *Dealer*."

The phone crashed in his ear. "Sonofabitch."

Maxine's thin lips dimpled at their corners. She looked as if he had confided in her. Well, why not? She was an intern from Ball State, tall, angular, boyish in a way, but the generous breasts made up for a multitude of sins. As a favor to Frank McGough, he had moved her to the head of the list of college kids wanting hands-on experience of state government. For a month Maxine would monitor the various aspects of a state senator's job. Not that Maxine was a typical coed. She had returned to college after an interlude of several years when her life crashed.

"A man?"

"What else?"

"You're divorced?"

"We never married."

"Ah." He put on an idiotic nonjudgmental smile.

Maxine came onto the floor of the assembly with him,

she was at his side throughout the day, she was enthralled by everything Boyd did or said. The aborted call to Willis Long was the first time since her internship began that Boyd had run into so much as a wrinkle on the surface of his work. He wanted to assure her that this was a real anomoly. He considered calling Willis back and chewing him out in turn, but the potentiality for coming out second best in such an exchange—the habit of catering to constitutents was deeply ingrained—decided against that. Instead, he began immediately to write an op ed piece, certain that Humphrey would run it first thing.

His theme was the temptation of constituents to misinterpret the phrase public servant. Too many voters thought that a senator was their personal voice in Indianapolis, committed to doing anything they suggested. The fallacy lay in overlooking the vast number of constituents with their conflicting desires, and the necessity finally for a senator to make hard decisions. The voters had to be consulted, their views registered, but since it was impossible to represent conflicting and multiple wishes, it was the senator's lonely task to make up his own mind and then submit to the judgment of the voters. Their judgment, not their vituperation. From time to time a constituent came along who regarded his representative as a whipping boy, a scapegoat. Boyd would not bore the reader by quoting the language the politician was sometimes subjected to. He was, he assured the readers of the *Wyler Dealer*, their good servant but his own conscience's first.

He liked it. Maxine loved it. She faxed it off to Humphrey and it appeared in the next issue. His sense of triumph was short-lived. Willis Long might have had his reply already written when Humphrey, in the interests of fairness, called the man and asked if he would like to reply to Senator Carlson's piece.

"What the hell did you do that for, Humph? I never mentioned the man's name."

"Boyd, our readers would see the connection between his earlier piece and yours."

"Thanks a helluva lot."

"I think you come out fairly well."

Fairly well! Willis referred to him as Bingo Boyd and Humphrey had put the phrase into the title of the piece—admittedly in quotation marks.

"He must be nuts," Maxine said sympathetically.

At the moment, Boyd considered all constituents demented. He began to tell Maxine stories about some of the troubles he'd had over the years. She was a receptive audience and clearly saw him as the hero of these exchanges. She had not known of the way the late Senator Young of Ohio had dealt with irate letters. "Dear ———, Some idiot sent me the enclosed letter and signed your name. I know you will want to do something about this outrage. Sincerely." Maxine's laughter throatily filled the office. Once he had begun, it was pleasant to go on. The secretaries left, the office closed, he and Maxine stayed on. It seemed perfectly natural to take her out to dinner.

She hung on his words throughout the meal. Fellow senators stopped by—the restaurant was a favorite of politicians—and Boyd introduced his intern. Foxley of Fort Wayne stepped out of range of Maxine's gaze and waggled his eyebrows. Boyd made a face but was suddenly aware of the fact that he was in a public place with an enthralled young woman. Immediately he was on his guard. For a politician, the path to doom passed through the loins. When he drove her to her boarding-house, she remained in the passenger seat after he had stopped, turned toward him, smiling radiantly.

"Thank you," she said as if the phrase had been minted for the occasion.

And then, impulsively, she leaned toward him and he kissed her cheek. The smell of her, her warm breath on his flesh, the swiftness of it, caught him unawares. She jumped out, slammed the door, and ran to the house, and he sat there with blood roaring in his ears.

There was a message from Frank McGough on his answering machine. Boyd made himself a drink, picked up the phone, and dialed Wyler, the country club.

"Nothing special," McGough said when he came on. "How's your bingo bill progressing?"

"If the vote were held today, I'd have two-thirds with me."

"Veto proof?"

"That's right."

McGough's appreciation of what he had accomplished was like a continuation of Maxine's receptivity. Why should he let an ass like Willis Long bother him when powerful men like Frank McGough were behind him?

"Do you know a man named Willis Long, Frank?"

"The guy who attacked you in the *Dealer*."

Boyd's heart sank. "Yes."

"Just a crank. The Indians now, they're something else. I half expect them to demand that we turn over the country club to them. No doubt their ancestors used to golf here. After today's round, I'd be happy to let them have the place." McGough laughed in a way that suggested he had used the joke before.

"How's my protégée doing?"

Boyd's mind was totally blank. He had no idea what McGough meant.

"Maxine Hassel."

"Oh, Maxine. She's doing fine! Bright girl, lots of help, I think she's learning a lot."

"Thank God. She's been through a lot."

"Is that right?"

"Nothing tragic, except to a young woman. Thwarted romance. You want me to do something about Willis?"

Do something? The phrase brought back the figure who had loitered in the background the time he and McGough went to Chicago to meet some clients who were contributing generously to the anti-bingo effort. All the while they talked that bodyguard had been in evidence. If that man were told to do something Boyd was sure he would do it.

"I'm just curious to know more about him," replied Boyd.

"No problem."

"I'll say hello to Maxine."

"No. No, don't do that. I don't want her to think you're doing her any special favors."

After he hung up, he wondered if Maxine's tragedy involved Frank McGough, but that was ridiculous. Just because she listened so attentively to him, deferred to him, did not mean she had a generic attraction to older men. Not that he himself was in the same age bracket as Frank McGough. He laughed aloud at the thought. Why, he doubted he was much more than a dozen years older than Maxine. Maybe fifteen.

"You should never have acknowledged his article in the first place," Wendy said when he called home.

"For that matter, you should never have inquired about his house."

"Oh, pooh. I learned that from you. Besides you know how swiftly Bel Air houses move."

"Are people talking?"

"About you? I hope so. Boyd, being controversial can't hurt you. Nothing Willis Long wrote has anything to do with you as a senator."

"I couldn't very well slough it off on you."

"You better not. How're things?"

"Come down for a few days."

"How I wish I could."

"Then do."

But there were deals afoot, there always were. He realized he wasn't that disappointed. Wendy's manner toward him was decidedly different from that of his staff. And Maxine's breathless interest in him was a tonic. Just talking on the phone with Wendy brought him down to earth, made his job seem humdrum. He sat back and tried to recover the euphoria he had felt dining with Maxine.

The phone rang. It was Maxine.

"I knew you were still up when I got a busy signal."

"Oh, I'm a night owl."

"Senator, I can't find an envelope I had with me. I wonder if I left it in your car."

"I'll go look."

"Oh, would you?"

"Of course. I'll call back."

It was in the backseat. She must have thrown it there to get it out of the way. He remembered that she had put her briefcase in back. He went upstairs and called her.

"A plain brown envelope? I have it. I'll bring it in tomorrow."

"Oh." A slight pause. "I don't suppose I could come by now and pick it up?"

"Of course."

After he hung up, he shook his head several times to rid it of the ridiculous thoughts that sprang into his mind. Troubled young intern drops by senator's apartment, he asks her to stay a while, she does . . .

The envelope was not sealed. He eased up the metal fastener, lifted the flap and looked inside. Some papers. The top one was blank. So were all the others. He carefully closed the envelope.

"I should have offered to bring it to you, Maxine."

"Oh, Senator." She stepped in and closed the door

behind her and now stood holding the envelope he had thrust into her hands.

"Call me Boyd. Pretty important stuff?" He nodded at the envelope.

She smiled prettily. "To me."

"I'm having a drink. Care for one?"

While waiting for her, he had loaded up the CD player and the apartment was filled with the strains of Montovani. She asked for bourbon on the rocks and when she sat, put the envelope on the coffee table. "So I don't forget it again."

"That was a very pleasant dinner we had," he said, when he settled down in a green leather chair of modern design.

"I find all this fascinating."

Well, it was. With Maxine he spoke of his ambitions matter-of-factly. She knew him only as he was and would not contrast his aspirations with his humble beginnings. He was after all from Wyler. Maxine betrayed no amusement at the mention of the town.

"It's right on the Tippecanoe, isn't it?

"Practically in Illinois."

"You were born there?"

"Born and raised."

She kicked off her shoes, drew her feet up on the couch, and held her drink in both hands as she listened to his account of an idyllic boyhood, going away to school but glad to return, wonderful people in Wyler, wonderful place to raise a family. He veered away from that. He didn't want any mention of Wendy in this conversation. He did tell Maxine of his real estate business. He wasn't the only one who'd returned to Wyler after being educated elsewhere. Humphrey, of course, though you could say his inheritance drew him back, but that was not the explanation for Andrew Broom or Frank McGough. Maxine gave no sign of recognition when he mentioned Frank. He would have liked to know how she had come to know, or be known by, the Wyler attorney.

As they talked, another version of his self observed the scene. He recalled the condescension with which he had discussed the foibles of his fellow lawmakers when they succumbed to the temptations of Indianapolis. He had expressed sympathy for their deceived wives. Now it occurred to him that in his own case the contrast was between Wendy and Maxine. Wendy was a fine woman, a good wife and mother, he had become a Catholic for her and he did not regret it for one moment. But she had long since lost the sense that what he did amounted to much or if it did then she just expected him to do well so what was the big deal? Maxine had all the freshness and wonder of a kid and yet, as he knew, she wasn't a kid. With any other intern there would not have been the dinner, there would not have been the invitation to a drink. When he freshened their drinks, she patted the couch beside her and rearranged her feet as he sat. He felt he was getting into bed with her.

Some hours later, in bed with Maxine, propped on an elbow, he looked down at her.

"What was in the envelope?"

"You wouldn't believe me."

"Tell me."

Her eyes seemed to go out of focus. "What my life was before I met you. Blank pages."

He gathered her into his arms as if she were a prize he had won.

TWENTY-EIGHT

"What do you know of this bastard Boyd Carlson?" Willis Long asked.

Gerald smiled. "Bingo Boyd?"

"Do you know what that lowlife did?"

Gerald had been admitted to Willis's house and without preamble the man got going on Boyd Carlson. As far as Gerald could see, the man's complaint was against Wendy Carlson, but there seemed little point in saying so. If nothing else, Gerald felt he was getting very rapidly on a confidential basis with Willis Long.

"I've got half a mind to consult a lawyer."

"Better do it with a full mind."

Willis laughed. He was a large pasty-faced man with a bald head that reflected light. The death of his wife had embittered him and Gerald was inclined to think Carlson was just a target of opportunity. Willis drank thirstily of his beer.

"Did you write that article yourself?"

"I wrote two."

144

"They were good."

"I was inspired. I haven't written anything longer than a letter since college."

"Mr. Long, I am a lawyer. I'm with Andrew Broom. Willis's brow darkened. "He's defending Blatz!"

"Only because he's certain Jerome Blatz did not kill your wife."

"But that's crazy. It was his shovel, he was there."

Of course it was crazy. Not that Gerald would have admitted that to Willis. He hesitated to admit it to himself. Andrew had a quixotic streak in him, a weakness for lost causes, but the pretense that Jerome Blatz was not guilty as charged stretched credulity.

"Is he serious?" Gerald had asked Susannah.

"About defending Mr. Blatz? Absolutely."

"Andrew claims he's innocent."

"Of course he's innocent!"

Until proven otherwise? Don't ask. Susannah would stick by Andrew until death and after; it was silly to expect her to share his doubts. If she did have the faintest hint of a notion that Andrew was embracing a lost cause, she would never say so.

To Willis Long he said, "If he's right, the one who did kill your wife is running around loose."

"You bet he is. He's out on bail."

"Can we talk about your wife?"

Willis opened his hands and his eyes lifted to the ceiling. "The poor woman is in the public domain now. Common property. Newspapers, television. Can you imagine what this does to the kids?"

"No. How are they taking it?"

"I sent them to my sister's in Joplin, Missouri. She'll keep them indefinitely. What does having your mother beat to death with a shovel do to you? I don't know. And at their ages? I've got half a mind to join them and stay there."

"Sell out?"

Willis couldn't hold his glare. "Don't tell Carlson."

"Tell me about your wife."

It was hard to believe that the deflated balloon of a man, hanging on to a can of beer as if it contained the meaning of life, was the same man who had written to the *Dealer*. Gerald had a bachelor's conviction that when he married he would remember every event and date of his courtship, that he would fashion a personal calendar on which to commemorate the highpoints of his love. Of course every day would be a highpoint. Willis wasn't sure how long he and Louise had been married or about the ages of his children. It seemed a fragile basis on which to erect his indignation with Boyd Carlson.

"Who were her friends?"

"We weren't very social. I work all day and I want to relax when I get home."

"I can understand that. What were her hobbies?" He looked at the portly Willis. "Did you bowl together?"

They didn't bowl, they didn't golf, they didn't go out to movies. Restaurants? Neither of them had been much for that. They hadn't acquired the habit because when the kids were young there had to be baby-sitters, adding to the expense.

"I'm a meat and potatoes man anyway," Willis said as if it were a badge of honor.

"Who were her women friends?"

It was dawning on Willis that he was providing a pretty bleak picture of his life with Louise.

"She was very popular in the neighborhood. And in school affairs."

"What school do your kids attend?"

Henry Shryker. "The woman next door works there. Ellen Parker. She and Louise were close friends."

Church? Our Redeemer Lutheran, when they went. A

few times a year. Good Protestants, but they didn't make a big thing of it. Gerald sensed there was no point pursuing that. Besides, he could ask the pastor.

He had resolved to throw himself wholeheartedly behind Uncle Andrew's decision that Jerome Blatz was innocent and it was incumbent on them to find the real killer. The sheriff was barely tolerant of the idea. He had made an arrest, Jerome had been arraigned, it had been established that his spade had been used to kill Louise Long. Why should he be intimidated by Andrew when he had the sheriff, the court, and the IBI backing him up? Not to mention the local newspaper.

When he first came to Wyler, Gerald found it impossible to take the *Dealer* seriously. He read the *Chicago Tribune*, from time to time the South Bend paper or the *Indianapolis Star*, but the *Wyler Dealer*? It came out three times a week, Monday, Wednesday, and Friday. Under the urgings of Susannah he did look at it and found it unintelligible. On the front page was a digest of wire service stories on national news, but inside was alien country and he had no compass. If you didn't know these people, what did it mean? But then he had come to know some of the people being written about and it began to make sense. One day he realized he had become a faithful reader. The influence of the *Dealer* locally would have been difficult to overestimate and if the paper was all they had to contend with, matters would have been simpler. The *Dealer*'s editorial assumption that Jerome Blatz was the slayer of Louise Long governed the paper's coverage of events, and influenced the local television station as well. "The putative slayer."

"Putative?"

Andrew smiled. "If they used 'alleged' readers would know the charge is unproven. Putative suggests a psychological aberration. . . . Did your wife know Jerome Blatz, Mr. Long?"

147

"Why do you ask that?" He sat up, fire in his eye, and there was a metallic sound as he crushed his beer can. It hadn't been empty and beer foamed over his fist.

"Did she?"

After a moment during which Gerald feared for his safety, Willis collapsed again and then he was blubbering. Louise, it appeared, had been an unhappy wife. Willis couldn't touch her but she was interested in every man she looked at.

"Did she have affairs?"

"I don't know. I saw Jack Parry with a woman and suddenly Louise appointed herself the guardian of hearth and home. She practically forced Ellen Parry into a divorce."

"You think she was down by the river to meet Jerome Blatz?"

"I don't know!"

He pushed himself back from the table and went to the answer the door. Gerald rose when he heard the voice. He was standing next to the kitchen table when Pascal Pence, the reporter, walked in.

"Someone to see you," Willis said.

"Oh no," she said. "I want to talk to you."

When Willis shook his head his jowls sloshed. His eyes were red. The poor sonofabitch. It seemed a merciful deed to get Pascal out of there. He effected this by whispering that he would tell her all.

"All what?" she asked, when they were walking toward their parked cars.

"All the news that's fit to print."

She looked betrayed. She stopped and turned toward the house as if to go back. But she must have realized that Willis Long would not open the door to anyone for a while.

"What's your favorite bar?" he asked her.

"The salad bar in Robertson's tearoom."

He managed to keep his smile. "I'll meet you there in fifteen minutes."

She did not say no. Her pensive look suggested that she thought she could pry anything newsworthy out of him over a tossed salad.

"Okay."

"I'll meet you by the spinach."

TWENTY-NINE

When Andrew Broom himself took a stool at her counter and ordered coffee Bonnie thought the best thing would be to pretend she didn't know who he was. He didn't expect her to.

"I'm Andrew Broom, an attorney. I'd like to talk with you."

"Go ahead."

"When are you through working?"

Her shift was just about to end. Somehow she felt he already knew that. They could talk in his car, which was parked outside, or they could go to his office. Whichever she preferred.

"What about?"

He smiled. "No point starting now." He toasted her with his mug and brought it to his lips.

He wanted to talk about Jack. She wasn't even surprised. As soon as the questions started she felt that she had been practicing evasive answers, knowing the time would come when the man defending Jerome Blatz would dis-

150

cover that Jack Parry had been down by the river just before the farmer got there. Jack said nobody could possibly have seen him—nobody except Louise Long, that is—so he wasn't worried. "Unless I should worry because I told you." As if she would ever turn on him!

"Louise Long came here to the truckstop, didn't she?"

"Did she?"

"Perfectly understandable, of course. She was a neighbor of Jack Parry and his wife. His former wife. You know Jack?"

"Of course I know Jack."

"You two are pretty serious, aren't you?"

"We're good friends."

"Jack is good friends with quite a number of women, isn't he?"

"Why do you say that!"

"His wife says it. It's why they divorced. Is he more faithful to you than he was to his wife?"

"What's your point?"

He had started the motor of his car, in order to run the air conditioner, and now Bonnie felt chilly even though it was eighty degrees outside the car.

"Was Louise Long one of Jack Parry's women?"

"If she was, I wouldn't know about it, would I?"

"Oh, I think so. Didn't you follow them around?"

"I did not! Look, I don't have to . . ." She tried to open the door but it was locked. She began looking desperately for a way to unlock it. "Let me out of here."

"In a case like this, Bonnie, when the wrong person has been arrested, we start looking around for someone who had a reason to kill Louise. Jerome had no reason. He had the dumb luck to be there and find the body, but he had no reason to kill her. He didn't kill her. But someone did. Someone who was furious that a homely little woman like Louise had stolen her man away. Would you like me to unlock that door?"

"Yes!"

There was a click and she pressed down on the handle and the door swung open. She looked at him, breathing heavily. "You're smart. I know that. You're smarter than I am. Someone's paying you to defend that farmer and you'll do anything you have to, but you're not going to pin it on me. I didn't do it. Maybe Jack had something to do with that woman and maybe he didn't. You're right. She wouldn't have been the first. And she wouldn't have been the last. I know that. His wife knew it. The difference is I'm willing to live with it."

And then she was out in the burning afternoon. She slammed the door shut and half blinded by the sun, stumbled toward the door of the restaurant. Then she changed course and went toward the cool cavern of the garage.

"Hey, Bonnie, how you doing?"

"Felix, where is Jack?"

"Geez, I don't know. Guy came asking for him ten, fifteen minutes ago but when I went for Jack I couldn't find him. I told him to look in the restaurant."

The man Felix described was Andrew Broom.

"What did he want?"

"I didn't ask. "

What was she doing asking dumb questions of Felix? If Jack wasn't here, chances were he had gone to her place. She left the shade and crossed the parking lot to where her car looked at the world through the big cardboard eyes in its windshield. That card was supposed to shut out the sun and keep her car cool but when she opened the door and reached in to remove the sun screen from the windshield she felt she was reaching into an oven for a pizza.

She left the door open as she settled behind the wheel and got the key in the ignition. The plastic edge of the seat was very hot against her legs. After starting the car, she pulled the door shut and rolled down the window. Andrew Broom still sat in his parked air conditioned car.

Bonnie ignored him. The lawyer already knew so much, he probably knew where she lived. But if she led him there and Jack was waiting for her . . . She pulled out of her space and immediately slammed on her brakes. A huge rig was moving majestically in from the highway, all chrome and white, its horn playing a song Bonnie couldn't identify. She waited for it to go by and then waited longer for a beaten-up van that came in right behind it and drove right into the garage. To her surprise Andrew Broom did not follow her from the lot.

THIRTY

Today was delivery day at the Indy Truckstop, but the hell with that, Jack was not going to come at the beck and call of Andrew Broom or any other goddam lawyer. Broom the local hotshot had confidently assured the press that his client was innocent and would not even be brought to trial.

"The truth will come out and come out soon."

Meaning he knew what the truth was. Jack left the garage at the far end, crossed the lot and disappeared into the weedy field beyond. He didn't know where he was going, only that he was going. Pollen as thick as heat stuck to his face and arms as he moved, swiftly and bent over, away from the truckstop. His car was parked in the truckstop lot, ahead was the looping exit from the interstate and, farther west, the river. The Tippecanoe. When he was a kid that had always been a refuge, the first destination on a summer outing, a never failing place of peace, away from adults.

He stopped and looked back at the truckstop. He was

surprised he was not farther away. Felix, the idiot, was running around between the garage and pumps, probably still looking for Jack Parry. "Someone here to see Jack Parry." he had called out. Someone. Jack recognized Andrew Broom when he saw him. He had slipped out of the cab, dropping soundlessly to the concrete, then headed out of the garage.

What the hell was he running from? He sat right down there in the dusty field, not minding the prickly weeds, not really feeling them, but smelling the sick-sweet odor of their purple and yellow flowers. He felt as he had when that lawyer of Ellen's talked to him. He didn't have a chance. He'd never had a chance. It had been a mistake to think that he could have a family like other men, buy a house in Bel Air, settle down. He'd been an outsider as a kid and he was an outsider still. He didn't really feel like Tommy's father, although of course he was. The kid was different, he belonged in that house, in that neighborhood. He was some kind of genius and that made him seem more of a stranger. Ellen was as bewildered by the boy as he was, but she was different too. She was a wife and mother. The best thing he had ever done for her and Tommy was to get the hell out of Bel Air. Her lawyer as much as said the same thing, but that didn't mean it wasn't true.

He knew now what Broom was thinking. The lawyer must have found out he'd been there by the river when Louise Long was stopped. How? It didn't matter how he found out. Maybe Bonnie had told them. Bonnie. He dug his hands into the soft soil and came up with handfuls of dirt that spilled from between his fingers like an hourglass. Who else knew? And then he thought. Tommy? He had gone in seach of Tommy and maybe the boy had seen him dig up the bag. If he had, he would have told Ellen and . . .

It was as if he'd already known all this when he had

slipped out of the garage and into this field. He could just wait here until Broom left. And then, carried on the hot air across the field from the truckstop, there came to him the melodious entry of the flashy rig that convoyed the truck with the stuff in it. The envelope of money was inside Jack's buttoned shirt. He'd been all ready for the delivery when Broom came and he took off on the run. What the hell could he do now? He knelt and watched Felix talking to the driver, who had gotten out of the delivery van. Felix was giving him a hard time. The driver could have decked Felix with a single punch, but something was wrong here and the driver knew it. He brushed past Felix and went out of sight but a minute later the big rig slid soundlessly out of the truckstop and there were two men in the cab. The battered truck sat in the garage where the driver had left it.

Andrew Broom, the now abandoned truck with the stuff concealed in the panel of its door—it seemed a very good time to keep on going. To hell with his own car. Jack continued through the field and came out on a service road that skirted the eastern side of the truckstop. He had to have a car. It took him five minutes to get back to the point where the road ran along the edge of the truckstop parking lot. What the hell, he had the pick of any car in the lot. He settled on a nondescript Honda with the driver's window a third open. He looped a shoelace over the lock, pulled it up, opened the door, and released the hood. A moment later he had it started.

He backed over the curbing that edged the lot and dipped into the ravine between the lot and road. For a moment he feared the car would get hung up over the ravine with the wheels not touching, but he goosed it and shot up out of the ravine and onto the road. A frantic horn sounded and he barely got the gear shifted and pulled the car out of the path of the station wagon. The terrified woman at the wheel went past and Jack felt the faces of her little passengers imprint themselves upon his mind.

But then he was barreling up the road, heading for Bonnie's. Everything was coming unglued and he had to pick up those safe deposit keys and clear out before the truck driver got word back to Chicago that things were all screwed up in Wyler.

THIRTY-ONE

When Bonnie the waitress drove away Andrew did not follow. He had come to the truckstop on a hunch and while talking with Bonnie was convinced he was onto something, but now he wasn't sure what that something was. His aim was to get Jerome off the hook by producing the one who had killed Louise Long and he was getting impatient. However improbable a suspect Jerome had seemed at first, people were getting used to him in the role of killer.

And no wonder. Awful things are done by ordinary people. "Like you and me," he had added, ruminating about this with Susannah.

"But why on earth would Jerome . . ."

So far as they knew, Louise was a stranger to him, but what if she weren't? They knew things about Louise now that they hadn't known before, things revealed when Willis Long had broken down, things that corroborated what Ellen Parry had said. Louise was a woman at a dangerous

age, convinced that just over the horizon of her life everyone else was having one helluva time and she was being cut
out of it. Living with Willis could not have been a barrel of
laughs. Her pursuit of Jack Parry suggested a woman
willing to make the first move. Was it unimaginable that she
had given Jerome Blatz an opening too? Louise was a little homely thing, Jerome was a weather-beaten grandfather,
but sex is a sardonic leveler. If he were the prosecutor,
Andrew knew he could make a more than plausible case
against Jerome. That shovel and his being there on the spot,
even though he had the excuse of meeting Lindel, would
make the task duck soup. But he was the defense lawyer,
not the prosecutor. Besides, he simply did not believe
Jerome was guilty. Guilty of disloyalty, double-dealing,
lying, yes, but not of murder.

His hunch about Jack Parry got a boost from what
Earl Waffle thought was a nutty call. Of course it was
one among several, but Andrew perked up when the
sheriff said one of the cranks mentioned Louise had
been seen at the truckstop.

"The Indy. The place out by the interstate."

Well, it did sound like the other call informing the
sheriff that Louise and Willis Long, while members of
the church, were not regular churchgoers.

But the truckstop was where Jack Parry worked, the
mechanic whose wife had divorced him because he
couldn't stop playing around. Louise was emerging as a
woman dying to play around. Her presence at the truckstop thus had almost syllogistic implications—if you
were subject to hunches. Checking out Jack Parry
revealed contradictory things. He was seeing Bonnie
regularly, though he never stayed overnight but
returned to his unit in the superannuated motel that
had been turned into rental apartments. And he attend-
ed church services twice a week.

"That man is saved," Grover Layton assured Andrew when he stopped by to talk with the preacher.

"Too bad about his marriage."

"God's gonna bring us as low as he has to to show us we can't do nothing by ourselves."

The walls of the tabernacle looked like beaverboard; fluorescent lights clung to the high ceiling like great insects. In the daytime, it was not an impressive place. The organ might have been picked up at the mall and the stage on which Layton preached buckled and echoed as they walked across it after their talk. Layton's office was in the back. From it he could emerge suddenly onto the stage when the place was full.

Gerald had provided details about the services, to the astonishment of Susannah and Andrew. A nephew caught up in born-again religion? It turned out that Gerald and Julie had used the services as a rendezvous.

"That's almost sacrilegious," Susannah said.

"Jack Parry is a regular there," Andrew reported when he returned from his interview with Grover Layton. He wasn't sure what it meant. "He tithes."

"You're lisping, Uncle Andrew."

Susannah made a face. "It means that he gives ten percent of what he earns to the tabernacle."

"Can't amount to much."

"It's the spirit, Gerald. If you'd pay attention when you attend you'd understand."

Funny that it was the tithing that Andrew remembered while he sat in his car in the truckstop parking lot, motor purring, the air conditioning making his vigil tolerable. Vigil? He had come to talk to Bonnie and then to Jack Parry and accomplished half of that. Jack seemed to be gone although the large-nosed young man with the narrow mouth professed to be surprised. Andrew sat in his car, reluctant to leave.

The big rig with the toodling horn swept majestically

into the truckstop and the contrast with the battered delivery van that followed was total. Andrew had the antic thought that the gaudy semi was running interference. The van turned into the garage, the driver hopped out and headed for the restaurant. But he was stopped by the same kid who had told Andrew Jack Parry was not there. The driver hesitated, looked around, then kept going. In a minute he came out of the restaurant, threaded his way among parked cars and trucks, and climbed into the cab of the gaudy semi. He was joined by the semi's driver, who came across the lot carrying a paper cup of coffee in a clawed hand, looking put upon and peeved. There was no musical horn when the big rig pulled out of the lot.

Andrew sat on. Minutes later a man emerged from beyond the parking lot, arising as if from the grave. Andrew realized it was Jack Parry. The mechanic looked around the lot, then went to a car and began systematically to break and enter. Very efficient. In less than a minute he had the motor going, slammed down the hood, jumped in and backed out of the lot, over the curbing, shot through the ditch and into the road, very nearly colliding with a passing station wagon. Andrew put his car in gear and went in pursuit.

Parry's stop at Bonnie's was a bit of a disappointment. His departure from the truckstop suggested a man on the run, but here he was, doing the obvious thing, heading for his girl's. Except that he left the car running in the driveway and didn't close the driver's door when he ran inside. Andrew half expected to see him come out with Bonnie and hit the road, but when he emerged he was still alone.

So absorbed was Jack Parry in what he was doing that Andrew felt little risk of being observed. Nonetheless, he kept at a discreet distance. Parry stopped at a branch bank where he produced a key for a safe deposit box, disappeared from Andrew's line of vision briefly, then slid the box onto the counter, business finished. On the way to his car, Jack patted his shirt. This giveaway made the mechanic seem almost innocent. There was a stop at another bank. While he waited, Andrew picked up his phone and dialed the sheriff.

"Earl, take this down. Dove gray Honda, license 576 V2A. It won't be reported yet, but it's stolen. The man who stole it is inside the Hoosier Saving branch out on Western. When you stop him you'll find he is carrying a lot of cash."

"This a joke?"

"It's no joke. I'll stick with him until you get here."

As Andrew put down the phone, Parry came out of the bank and hurried to his car. After he started it, he just sat there. Andrew watched him in his rearview mirror. Parry's head was ducked down, as if he were counting money. But then, head still down, the Honda began to move. Fast. It came right at Andrew's car, gathering speed, and instinctively Andrew crouched in his seat. The Honda hit his Jaguar with a hell of a bang and the impact set the car in motion. Andrew had been thrown sideweays, the seat belt not preventing his head from banging against the window. Meanwhile his car was pushed kitty-corner across the lot until there was another jolt and bang as he was jammed into another car.

The last sight he had of Jack Parry, the man was clearing the box hedge that bordered the bank parking lot and sprinting between two houses and then he was gone.

THIRTY-TWO

Jack Parry made Pascal feel a little like Pygmalion in reverse. It was difficult to believe a man that good-looking was not intelligent as well. He couldn't be just the caricature of the crude macho man he pretended to be. That seemed a shared joke they could laugh over when they had the date he asked for.

Oh, why kid herself? Even if he was just a good-looking mechanic from the truckstop who thought he was God's gift to women she probably would have gone out with him. Social life in Wyler made Bloomington seem a veritable whirl by comparison. On campus Pascal had hung out with a gang, men and women, not really paired off, all of them looking beyond Bloomington to the great real world. In Wyler Pascal was still looking beyond. Humphrey owned the paper and that made it different for him. After several lunches with the publisher during her first months on the paper, she had imagined what it would be like to marry him and settle down in Wyler. Of course she'd stay on the paper. They'd be a

163

husband-and-wife team. Wyler would be transformed because she would be. But that was a fantasy she had let go and not reluctantly. Humphrey seem to lack any shred of romanticism. He was aware of her as a woman, she could feel it, but he seemed unable to put it into words. She could have made it easier for him but that was too much like making the first move. He was a good-looking man, in a rough-hewn sort of way, and of course he owned the paper.

Gerald Rowan too had loomed as eligible until Pascal saw the lay of the land with Julie McGough. That country club crowd made her feel as poor as a church mouse and it was a relief to feel mildly condescending to Jack Parry. She still found it incredible that she had succumbed to him on their first and only date. His conversation was largely about automobiles and his son, but everything he said had the effect of bringing them closer together. He had a wonderful voice and spoke softly so that she leaned toward him to hear. They'd sat side by side on a banquette in the seedy roadhouse he took her to; his leg was warm against hers; when coffee came he put his arm on the back of the banquette and she didn't object. It was that kind of place. When he took her home he came right in with her without being asked. That they were going to bed seemed another foregone conclusion. And they went to bed.

Even now, remembering, Pascal opened her mouth a little and breathed deeply. She should feel ashamed to have been so easy a conquest, she should feel remorse for violating her own moral code. She should despise a man who saw her simply as a fugitive bed mate. What she preferred to do was think of it as a fantasy that had come true, a single perfect event without prelude or sequel, what it was and nothing else, hers to cherish as a memory. Whatever condescension she had felt for Jack beforehand, he had conferred on her self-confidence as a woman. That had been his gift, whatever his motives. Let him look on it as a conquest if he wanted to, for her it had been a sublime excursion out of character.

Having spinach salad with Gerald Rowan in Robertson's tearoom to find out what Willis Long had told him might have been different if there hadn't been Jack. And if she didn't know about Julie McGough.

"Willis says his wife was a loose woman," remarked Gerald.

Long had been a terror for over a week, attacking Boyd Carlson with zest and effect, indignant at official and journalistic speculation about his wife. It made no sense that he would now break down and say such things and Pascal said so.

"I didn't say it made sense. It's what he said. As a matter of fact, it does make a sort of sense. Long mentioned the guy who used to live next door. Willis saw him with another woman, told Louise, who told the wife and more or less pressured her into going for a divorce, after which Willis thinks Louise made a play for the guy."

"The guy?"

"Jack Parry."

On her plate greenery made a grotesque still life—oil stood viscously on her spinach, covered the upper hemisphere of a love apple tomato like global meltdown. Putting such vegetation in her mouth seemed a strange rite. Gerald was going on about Jack Parry, his divorced wife, his son, the girl he had at the truckstop.

"How do you know all these things?"

His brows danced. "Ve haf informants." He leaned forward. She sat back. "Another waitress at the truckstop. Probably jealous of Jack Parry's girl. She told us Louise had been hanging around there. This Parry is some stud."

His manner invited droll comments on the lower classes. It was an invitation she would have accepted, normally. It was an occupational hazard to regard people as oddities whose main reason for being was to provide incredible tales for the press. As a lawyer, Gerald would have an even dimmer view of the race. For the first time, Pascal felt really embarrassed by the fact that she had made love with Jack Parry and become just another of his one-night stands. Would she end up in a catfight with a truckstop waitress and frustrated matrons from Bel Air?

Gerald apparently detected nothing in her manner and settled back to discuss in a philosophical mode the task Andrew Broom faced in defending Jerome Blatz. The wider net they were throwing would do the trick, he was sure of that. What Pascal began to fear was that the wider net would settle over her as well.

She left work early, having borrowed liberally from Gerald's summary to write a story. The local news of the day did not interest her. Because of the late lunch with Gerald she was not hungry. She had half a mind to hit the hay early and get a twelve-hour sleep. It wasn't that she was tired so much as that she wanted oblivion. She did not want the thoughts to form that Gerald's joshing remarks about Jack would almost certainly prompt if she gave them the least opportunity. She might even take a sleeping pill, to bring on unconsciousness more quickly.

The door of her apartment was locked but as soon as she let herself in, she knew she was not alone. Her back to the closed door, she reached behind her for the handle, wanting to open it again. Her whole body seemed to have become a sensor as she strained to hear.

"Pascal?"

My God, it was Jack! He stood in the shadow of the hallway so immobile that she might not have noticed him for a moment more if he had not spoken. "What are you doing here? How did you get in?"

But it was not indignation that these words expressed. Surprise of course, but delight as well. The drapes were pulled, she had not turned on any light, the apartment seemed unreal, occupying a time and place outside the ordinary. It was very much as it had been when they had come here from the roadhouse. Jack came silently across the room and she tried to remain where she was but before he was halfway to her, she began to move toward him.

It could not be called rape when she cooperated as she did. Pascal was an accomplice in her own humiliation when, clinging to one another, feeling as if they were in a sack race at a picnic, they stumbled down the hall and onto her bed where he took her with an odd mixture of violence and tenderness. Afterward, he lay on his back, staring at the ceiling, breathing noisily through his open mouth. She half hoped he was not done with her.

"I'm leaving town. I want you to come with me."

"Where are you going?"

"I don't know." He turned his head and stared at her. "I need you with me. You need me."

She felt an impulse to ask why he had not called her after their date, but that would have sounded childish in the circumstances. Tugging her twisted clothing into some sort of shape, she fought the feeling of being flattered by his invitation. Or was it an order? She was surprised and frightened by the docility he elicted from her. This wasn't her! She was damned if she was going to be anyone's love slave, let alone a truckstop mechanic's. But it was impossible, looking at his perfect features, the blond hair, to think of him as beneath her.

"Why do you want to leave Wyler?"

A little crooked grin. "I want to stay alive."

"Has someone threatened you?"

"They don't have to." He rolled onto his side and spoke with urgency. "There isn't time to explain now. Where's your car?"

"I don't have a car. Not of my own. It belongs to the paper."

"You don't have a car." He said it in disbelief. He pushed away, stood and began to buckle his belt. An expression of tenderness flitted across his face as he looked down at her. "I am going to leave something here, okay? I put it in your freezer."

"What?"

"Don't ask. It's better that you don't know."

"I have to know." She went into the kitchen and pulled open the refrigerator door. In the freezer, in Ziploc storage bags, she found the money, packages of bills, twenties, fifties, hundreds. She put the bags back, stacked an ice cream carton and some frozen pork chops in front of them. It's his life savings, she told herself. Cash he has been putting away. She shut the refrigerator and without looking at him went back to the bedroom. He came with her, they sat on the bed, his arm about her. He shook his head in disbelief.

"I was sure you had a car."

"Jack, even if I did . . ." Her voice drifted away. She could not look at him. She did not want to know where that money had come from. She did not want to be privy to his plans. She wanted him to go. As if he could read her thoughts, he stood.

"I'll be in touch."

She stayed in the bedroom. He went into the kitchen as if he meant to leave by the back door, but he changed his mind and swiftly passed her door on his way to the living room. She waited until she heard the door close, then leaped from the bed and hurried to it. She locked the door and put on the chain.

On the local news she saw the clip taken at the parking lot of the branch bank, four cars smashed together, one a very expensive Jaguar. "This," the reporter said, laying his hand on the crumpled fender, "is the automobile of local attorney Andrew Broom. And this is the car that was driven by the man now being sought by the sheriff. The car was stolen from the Indy Truckstop earlier. The suspect escaped over that hedge, running between those houses." And then a close-up of Jack Parry filled the screen and Pascal cried out in anguish.

She catnapped through the night, half expecting Jack to come back. What other refuge did he have? In the morning she looked at herself in the mirror, then looked away. She had aged five years since yesterday. Ages had passed since she'd entered her apartment and Jack had come toward her out of the shadows. She shut her eyes at the memory. And then, humming, she prepared her breakfast.

Before leaving for work, she checked the freezer of her refrigerator. The Ziploc bags were gone.

THIRTY-THREE

"How did you get in!"

Jack took a key from his shirt pocket and held it up.

"You were supposed to give me all your keys."

"You could have changed the locks."

Ellen had never even thought of it. It was surprising that Louise hadn't. Louise was so full of advice when Ellen's marriage crashed. Ellen should have suspected her neighbor's motives, Jack always had and he had been right. Imagine Louise, after all but forcing Ellen to divorce Jack, chasing after him, hanging around the truckstop.

"What do you want?"

"Just stopping by."

"Jack, I heard the news. The police are looking for you. Sooner or later, they'll come here."

He shook his head. "I don't think so. Where's Tommy?"

"He's still at school."

"When do you expect him back?"

"Jack, what are you going to do?"

"Start a new life. Isn't that what divorce is for? Maybe you should do the same."

"No."

He nodded and came close to her, put his hand on her arm. "Poor Ellen."

"I'm not poor Ellen!"

"You have been ever since you met me, kiddo."

She turned away, unable to hold back the tears. There had been a time once when their life together had been fine, as much as anyone could ask. Ellen felt now that she could have tolerated his quickies if only she and Tommy and Jack had remained together. Tommy needed a father. And Jack needed Tommy. But it was all too late for that. The police would find him sooner or later.

"Too bad about Louise."

She swung on him. "Jack, you had nothing to do with that, did you?"

"No!" He seemed genuinely shocked.

When Tommy came home, he showed no surprise to find his father there. It was difficult to know what the boy had made of the divorce, of living alone with his mother and seeing his father only from time to time. Jack and Tommy went back to his room and Ellen listened to them talking, Jack laughing, it sounded so normal. She was standing there with a little smile on her face when the front doorbell rang. There was scurrying behind her as she went to the door. The men standing on the doorstep frowned at her and then came inside.

"Where is he?"

But they didn't wait for an answer, one of them flipping his wallet open and shut, as they went by. Hugging herself, Ellen watched them as they looked in the dining room and kitchen and then went down the hall. One of them went into Tommy's room and then let out a yelp. "Jesus!" he shouted and it almost sounded like a prayer.

171

But it was drowned out by the clacking clutter of falling bones.

The man came out of the room, kicking plastic bones before him. There was only the basement left. Jack was coming up the stairs to meet them.

"Good afternoon, gentlemen."

"FBI."

"You're kidding." Again there was the opening and shutting of the wallet. "Well, well." Jack looked almost flattered to have rated such attention. Tommy followed him up from the basement, his eyes wide. The smile faded from Jack's face and he turned away.

"Let's go."

Tommy noticed the bones of his skeleton scattered in the hallway and was busy collecting them when Jack went out the door in custody. Watching them put Jack into the car and drive away with him, Ellen had the funny thought that Louise would have loved to witness such an exciting event. She herself felt devoid of feeling. Thank God Tommy had taken it as well as he had. But when she went down the hall to his room, she found him lying face down on his bed. She sat beside him and put her hand on his back. She tried to think of something to say. Finally, silence seemed the best way for them to communicate.

The sound of the doorbell made Tommy spring from the bed. He ran to the front door and pulled it open. Did he expect his father to be back? The man wore a Stetson hat and a sad expression as he looked past Tommy to her.

"Sheriff Earl Waffle, ma'am. He here?"

"They've already arrested him."

He pushed back the hat. "I don't understand you."

"The FBI," Tommy said, almost proudly. "They came for my dad."

"I'll use your telephone, if I may," the sheriff said.

Ellen listened to the sheriff talk, his voice merely impatient at first, then becoming angry. Gradually it dawned on Ellen what he was saying. The men who had taken Jack away were not from the FBI.

"But who were they?" she asked the sheriff.

"That's what I mean to find out."

THIRTY-FOUR

At the branch bank, Andrew Broom was offered a lift in a sheriff cruiser, Hank Skifton at the wheel.

"Let's detour to the truckstop, Hank."

Hank frowned. The sheriff had just instructed him to take Andrew to his office and now he was being given a different destination. This objectively insignificant dilemma loomed like a moral mountain on the featureless moonscape of Hank Skifton's mind.

"The truckstop?"

"On the way to my office."

"But your office is downtown."

"That's right. Turn here, Hank." They discussed the problem all the way to the truckstop, Hank dutifully following Andrew's directions while pondering the wisdom of following his directions.

Felix, crouched beside the van, checking tire pressure with a gauge, looked up when they approached. "He ain't back, mister." The mechanic took in Hank, resplendently uniformed, and tried to show contempt but it was envy that shone on his greasy face.

"Whose van is this?"

"Jack Parry should be working on it."

Andrew went around the truck, followed by Skifton and Felix. Given its apparent condition, it was surprising the van was still operational.

"It looks like it needs a lot of work."

"Jack Parry can work miracles," Felix said. "Why, he can sit behind the wheel of a vehicle, eyes shut, listening, and tell you more about that engine than a squad of people poking around under a hood."

Andrew opened the driver's door, found the inside of the cab reasonably clean, and stepped up and settled behind the wheel. The keys were in the ignition. He turned and looked down at Skifton.

"Hank, check the plates on this van, will you?"

"Something wrong?"

"Well, the man who drove this van into the garage left about forty-five minutes ago in another truck. A big flashy rig with a musical horn."

"The Good Humor Man!" Felix grinned. "That's what we call him. The Good Humor Man." He frowned. "What do you mean, this driver left?"

"He skeddadled when you told him Jack Parry wasn't here."

"They'd told him inside Jack was on duty. Well, he was but he left. Just what I told the man."

"And the driver promptly got out of here." Skifton took down the license number of the van, then went to the squad car to contact the sheriff.

Andrew pulled the van door closed, turned the ignition key, and sat there with his eyes closed. Jack Parry must be part con man to have convinced others that all he had to do was listen to an engine to diagnose its ailments. Andrew took his hands from the wheel and placed them on the seat. Outside, Felix banged on the door. Andrew rolled down the window.

"You gotta attach the hose to the exhaust before you run an engine in here."

"Right."

He turned the key and reached for the door handle. Felix's pounding had dislodged some gunk from the door and a silvery screwhead sparkled in the sun, not rusted like the others holding the panel in place. Andrew took out his nail clippers and easily removed the rusty-looking gunk from the other screwheads.

"Got a screwdriver, Felix?"

The tool he handed up had a bit an inch wide. "Got a smaller one?"

Felix unclipped a small screwdriver with a yellow plastic head from his shirt pocket. Perfect. Andrew loosened the top screws of the panel and looked inside. He asked Felix for a flashlight and when he saw the package, pushed the panel tight against the door and got down from the driver's seat. He had taken the keys with him. He locked the door of the cab and went out to the cruiser.

"Sheriff's out somewhere," Skifton said.

"Get the state police."

"Oh, I'm not gonna do anything like that, Mr. Broom."

Andrew turned and ran toward the restaurant. On a public phone he got hold of the state police headquarters twenty miles east on the interstate, identified himself and told the communications officer to send a trooper as quickly as possible.

"What's the nature of the problem, Mr. Broom?"

"Drugs."

Back at the cruiser, Skifton had established contact with the sheriff. He reached the mike out to Andrew.

"A helluva thing, Andrew. Parry's ex-wife said the FBI had been to the house and arrested her husband." Earl made a disgusted sound.

"He was there?"

"Not when I got there. There ain't no FBI in on this, is there?"

"Earl, the state police are on their way to the truckstop . . ."

"The state police! What in the name of God is going on? FBI, state police, what else, the Marines? Tell me what the hell is going on."

"If you hurry you could get here first." He handed the microphone back to Skifton, returned to the public phone inside the restaurant, and called Susannah.

"Andrew! Gerald says you've been in an accident."

"Well, my car has. I'm all right. How about coming out here with your car?"

"Where are you?"

He told her and then took a stool at the counter and ordered coffee. A carrot-haired woman with a color-coded snood waited on him.

"Bonnie's gone."

"Who're you?" The name 'Phyllis' was imprinted on the tag pinned to what would have been the breast of a better endowed woman.

"Bonnie and I's friends. She left. Jack Parry left. What's happening?"

"I'll tell you when you bring my coffee."

"I wish I could talk."

She poured his coffee and hurried away, her crepe soles sticking and unsticking as she went. The busy noisy truckstop restaurant was not the ideal place in which to do it but Andrew sipped his coffee and considered the events of the past hour, the past weeks since Jerome Blatz had come to him to discuss a surprising offer for forty acres along the Tippecanoe. Foxy Jerome

177

had been about to double-cross his fellow landowners, to say nothing of his lawyer, when he had been caught up in another matter, the finding of the murdered Louise Long.

Andrew's principal task was to defend Jerome against the charge that he killed Louise Long, a task he portrayed to Gerald and Susannah as easy. And in many ways it should be easy, always on the assumption that Jerome Blatz was, as he insisted and Andrew believed, innocent. But someone was guilty and that someone might very well have been Jack Parry.

Andrew had all the proof he needed that Jack Parry was a determined man. He must have skipped out of the garage when he heard Andrew asking for him and now it seemed that he had screwed up a rendezvous with the driver of that van. Andrew was certain that the truckstop was the place where drugs were coming into Wyler. It would start with marijuana, bad enough, but not all that worrisome, because there were so many free-lance growers and dealers anyway, but free-lancers wouldn't use a drop like the one Jack Parry was apparently involved in. The mechanic was a link between the truckstop and the land along the Tippecanoe, but Andrew was darned if he could see what it added up to. Chances were that the arrest of Jack Parry had been a staged rescue. When it became clear that the men who took Jack away were not FBI, there were several possible explanations. He had been kidnapped or he had been escorted to safety.

"Phillipa Cooper is kicking up a fuss about a stolen skull," Susannah said when she arrived.

Andrew laughed, startling his wife.

"I wonder what kind of reaction 'thigh bone' would have gotten?"

"I'll show you later."

The reminder of the missing skull and Phillipa's effort

to stage a reburial ceremony came as comic relief, but shortly afterward Andrew's attitude altered. Earl Waffle, with the state police looking on, removed the panel from the van door and brought out the package.

"Whose truck is this?" Waffle asked.

Felix stepped back. "Don't ask me. Your deputy was checking on it."

"It's not stolen," Skifton said, stepping forward.

Taking possession of the van and the package, presumably cocaine, made up a bit for the anger Earl felt at missing Jack Parry. On the drive to the truckstop, siren shrieking, he had communicated by radio with the FBI and been treated to a stream of ambiguities. They would send a man to discuss the matter with Earl Waffle but were unable at this time, and in this manner, to answer his inquiry. And why was there a siren going in the background?

Pascal Pence of the *Dealer* arrived and Susannah and Andrew left. On the radio, the plaintive voice of Phillipa was heard, speaking in shocked tones of the desecration involved in stealing the remains of a Native American. "Of any American, of anyone, for that matter, but to desecrate the remains of a Native American after all the humiliations our people have suffered from the occupying majority is particularly horrible."

Phillipa spoke reverently, almost lovingly of the skull, which bore the mark of injustice on its very forehead. The hole through which the bullet of the massacring white victors had entered.

"I can't believe this interest in skulls," Susannah said.

"And now for thigh bones."

Susannah gave a little yelp and moved to get out of range of his pinching fingers.

THIRTY-FIVE

When a monogamous man like Boyd Carlson has an affair he is bound to think of regularizing the situation. He must put away his wife and offer his hand in marriage to Maxine.

"Don't be silly. I don't want you to ruin your life."

"But this isn't fair to you."

"Don't underestimate yourself." And she moved her warm body closer to his. He caught his breath with excitement even as he hoped he was not expected to rise again to the occasion. He had a vivid image of their ages, his numbers above hers, crying out for subtraction and the revelation of the difference. To say he could be her father was a cliché; it was also false. Older brother, maybe, or a young uncle. He could not believe his luck that he could enjoy her with impunity. But that is what she was clearly telling him.

In the following days, his manner changed subtly, clear to anyone who worked closely with him. Boyd

Carlson had become a worldly man, as sophisticated as his character permitted, more tolerant of the foibles of others now that he was reacquainted with his own. His anti-bingo campaign no longer made his pulse race with righteousness and he was more than receptive to Andrew Broom's suggestion that promised a different and more flexible crusade.

"The land is public now, providing access to the river, but this can be replaced easily. A bill to return this land to Cooper's people would be both appropriate and well received," Andrew explained.

"It's state land?"

"That's right. More accurately, it is an Indian burial ground wrongly expropriated by our forebears." A pause. "Do you have any Indian blood in you?"

"No!"

"Good, then your bill will not seem self-serving. Not that it won't help erase your image as Bingo Boyd."

That did it. Boyd contacted his party leader, had the resolution tacked onto a bill that had overwhelming bipartisan support, and twenty-four hours after Andrew Broom's phone call a wedge of riparian land had been deeded back to Cooper's tribe—it was thus vaguely stated in the legislation—by the state of Indiana. He took Frank McGough's call in an exuberant mood.

"What the hell are you doing down there, Carlson? Is it true that you propose to give land back to the Indians?"

"The property in question is negligible in size, Frank. Apparently once a burial grounds. You know how sensitive we've all had to become to the rightful claims of Native Americans."

"Don't talk that crap to me, Boyd. I was born in Wyler. I'm as much a Native American as anyone else. Where is this land?"

Details of his coup would not yet have appeared in the *Wyler Dealer*. How had the news gotten so quickly to Frank McGough?

"Down by the Tippecanoe."

There was a frigid silence on the line and then McGough asked in a low steady voice. "Exactly where?"

"It's state land, Frank. It presently gives public access to the river."

"Jesus H. Christ, Boyd, are you out of your mind? Let me explain a few things to you."

McGough spoke rapidly and with clipped articulation of the men in Chicago who had contributed to the anti-bingo campaign. Did Boyd know why such powerful people had decided to contribute to the coffers of an obscure Indiana state senator? Because they were clients of Frank McGough, that's why.

"I am representing them in the purchase of land along the river, Boyd. If the state is willing to release its claim on that public access, my clients will buy it."

"But what has river land got to do with bingo?"

"Do you get the newspapers down there in Indianapolis, Boyd? Have you been following what our sister state has been doing with her waterways? Riverboat gambling, Boyd. It's a tax collector's dream. First we knock out bingo, then we follow Illinois into this very lucrative revenue enhancer. I thought you got the picture a long time ago. We don't want some goddam Indian burial ground cramping the development of that land."

Boyd, made bullish by his recent bouts between adulterous sheets, grew increasingly irate as he sat through Frank McGough's condescending lecture. This was altogether too much like the letters of Willis Long. Long might pin on him the label of Bingo Boyd but what could Frank McGough do to him? After all, on this he had the powerful support of Andrew Broom. He was no party to whatever pact Frank McGough had entered into with his Chicago friends. If attacking bingo had answered to something deep in Boyd's Puritan heart, the thought of gambling boats on the Tippecanoe filled him with disgust. His crusade against bingo was now revealed as a ploy, the first stage of a plan to legalize gambling of the most ruinous sort. Boyd had overcome his distaste for the state lottery, it would have been political suicide to oppose it, but the thought that he had been cast in the role of champion of legalized gambling put steel in his spine.

"You listen to me, Frank McGough. I am withdrawing my support for the anti-bingo bill. I am going to release all pledges to support it. I'll be damned if I'll be party to this scheme."

After a pause, Frank McGough said cheerfully, "I'll forget you said that, Boyd. You're too good a politician to commit suicide."

"Are you threatening me?"

"Physically? Don't be an idiot. You're a family man. We have to think of your wife."

"What are you talking about?"

"Maxine."

Boyd Carlson's legs felt rubbery and his chest constricted. He sat holding the phone long after it went dead, staring straight ahead, suddenly seeing what he had not seen before. Frank McGough had introduced a Trojan Horse into his staff and the invader had done her job with skill.

THIRTY-SIX

When Jerome Blatz shuffled into the kitchen it was clear to Andrew Broom that this ordeal had chastened his client considerably. After a lifetime of imagined misfortune, Jerome found that the real article robbed him of appetite, made his bowels irregular, soured his stomach beyond the reach of Arm & Hammer. But hope flickered when he saw Andrew.

"Have you found out who did it?"

"Not yet, Jerome."

Skifton had stopped by the farm and told Jerome about Jack Parry, a garbled account which Andrew had no desire to correct. If Jack Parry was destined to take Jerome's place as the accused, he first had to be found. The circumstances of his departure filled Andrew with foreboding. All the more so since he had talked to Tommy Parry about the skull he had found near the river.

"Right here," Tommy said, placing an index finger on the center of his forehead. "It was a bullet hole."

There was no point in questioning the basis for this certitude. Andrew shared it and on a flimsier basis—the say-so of Phillipa and now Tommy.

Phillipa had taken the bullet hole to be evidence of the unjust treatment of her adopted people by white assassins and was not deterred by the fact that a number of Native American groups had raised objections to her exploitation of their grievances, questioning her right to speak for any tribe. But thus far such statements had fallen short of repudiation. And then Phillipa called to tell him the skull was gone.

"Clark?"

Her husband's enthusiasm for Phillipa's crusade was muted at best, and it was conceivable that Clark had gotten rid of the skull. He found it difficult to sleep in the mobile home with that grinning companion, even when it was stored in a box in the kitchen. Phillipa had been sure Clark had thrown out the skull, but when Andrew went to see her, she had changed her mind. Her right eye was purplish and her lip swollen.

"You're sure?"

"If he had he would have taken credit for it."

Andrew wasn't so sure. Who would have known where the skull was? Who would have wanted to steal it?

They walked across to the Bison and found Clark in his office behind the bar where Andrew argued Phillipa's case with her dour companion.

"The state has deeded the property to you, and my client Jerome Blatz is prepared to add the adjacent forty acres to the parcel."

"Give it to them?" Jerome had bleated when Andrew made the suggestion. No doubt he was thinking of the amount Bink Phillips and Wendell stood to make by selling their pieces of riverfront land to Frank McGough's Chicago clients.

"That land has turned into a jinx for you, Jerome. Let it go."

"I ought to get compensation from the state . . ."

"Jerome, do what I ask. Otherwise I'm not sure I'll be able to clear your name."

"What the hell has my land to do with that?"

"The body was found on your land."

In the end, Jerome agreed, reluctantly, and now Andrew found himself trying to persuade Clark Cooper to fall in with Phillipa's plan for a fitting ceremony at the recovered burial grounds.

"How do we know that's where the grounds were?"

"It's where the skull was dug up by that boy," Andrew said.

"But the skull is gone!"

"You don't have to sound so gleeful about it!" Phillipa said. "We don't need it. We'll have a ceremony anyway. To drive off the evil spirits brought on by the white man."

"It would be better if we had a reburial too," Andrew said.

"Of course it would. But we can't."

"I think we can."

Phillipa listened eagerly as he laid out his plan for exhumation. Students from various state colleges who had experience in archaeological digs would be brought in for the event and, of course, deputized by Clark to act on behalf of his tribe. With appropriate care and reverence, remains would be unearthed and then reburied with appropriate pomp and circumstance.

"What if that ain't the place?" Clark asked sullenly.

"Of course it's the place."

"Look, you gonna get a lot people there, all kinds of publicity. What happens when they dig around and don't find nothing? What happens then, huh?" For Clark this amounted to eloquence.

"That's a risk we have to take," Andrew said, and Phillipa straightened her shoulders.

"What risk are you taking?"

On the way back to the office, he pondered Clark's question. Risks? Let me count them. I may be driving important investors from Wyler. I may make myself a laughingstock, aiding and abetting a dubious ritual by would-be Native Americans which will bring down on the town the wrath of legitimate tribes with genuine grievances. Not even Humphrey would keep that out of the paper or conceal the culprit. But these risks were as nothing beside the very real possibility that he would be checkmated by Frank McGough.

THIRTY-SEVEN

Pascal donned her professional persona and gathered reactions to the dramatic events at the Indy Truckstop that ended when one of the mechanics had rammed his stolen car into the pursuing Andrew Broom's Jaguar and then took off on foot. The waitresses were far less cooperative than before, no doubt because of the discovery of the drugs in the panel of the van abandoned in the truckstop garage, abandoned, so the theory went, because Jack Parry, the intended recipient, had disappeared. Bonnie shrugged and seemed ready to deny she had ever even heard of Jack Parry. Ah well, Holy Week was right around the corner. I know not the man. An attempt to get Bonnie talking by changing the subject to the discovered skull, her brother, and his zealot wife was unsuccessful. Phyllis was eager to talk but said she didn't dare with Bonnie looking on.

"Are you afraid of her?"

The birdlike eyes bulged. "She and Jack were like that," she whispered, crossing one finger over another.

It did Pascal's ego little good to sight in on Bonnie over the rim of her coffee cup. My rival? The waitress was old enough to be her mother. But then Jack had never pretended to be discriminate. Pascal's breath caught at the memory of her helplessness before him. When she left, she waved at Bonnie—a little camaraderie, their sorority's secret sign?—but the waitress ignored her.

Experience as a journalist had altered Pascal's sense of the news. Once she would have thought of it as an accurate, reasonably complete account of important events. At the moment, it was the incompleteness of the Jack Parry story that made her almost cynical toward her craft. It wasn't simply that she knew and others did not where Jack had gone after he ran from the parking lot of the bank. He had wanted her to run away with him! Of course in the snuggling dark warmth of her bed, enfolded in his arms, she could imagine stepping completely out of character and speeding away in a stolen car with Jack. Until she remembered why he had come to her. There was safety in her apartment, time to think. He had thought she owned a car, one he could use. Asking her along might have been meant as a reward. But his interest in her waned after he learned she didn't own a car. He had spent the night, why not? Pascal pounded on the steering wheel of the company car, but the indignation and shame she should have felt would not come.

When she walked into Andrew Broom's reception room, her mood was equivocal. Her full rust skirt and orange blouse lent grace to her movements and she had as many chains around her neck as an Orthodox prelate. The outfit made her feel beautiful but the feeling did not make her happy. Discussing Jack Parry in the vicinity of Gerald Rowan was something she would have preferred to postpone indefinitely.

Andrew would see her in a few minutes. Meanwhile Susannah Broom took her in to Gerald, stepping aside to let Pascal enter the office.

"Ta ta," she said, half mocking the formality of her entry.

"Stop! Stay right there." He rose from behind the desk, his face screwed into a studious expression. "Now, turn slowly, counterclockwise. Slowly!"

Pascal turned but there was nothing behind her. She came around three hundred and sixty degrees. Gerald's expression had changed.

"Lovely. Absolutely lovely."

And Susannah, in the doorway, nodded agreement and then was gone.

"You idiot," Pascal cried, but Gerald, all business now, extended his hand. She ignored it and stood before the desk. "What is your reaction to the events at the Indy Truckstop?"

"You should ask Andrew. It was his Jag that got totaled."

When Andrew joined them, he was more ebullient than Pascal had ever seen him. The Jaguar? He was due for a new one anyway and his insurance covered whatever loss he would suffer.

"Why were you following him?"

"Two reasons. One, I had gone out there to talk to him. Second, when he couldn't be found, I was waiting in my car and I saw him sneak into the lot, steal a car, jump a ditch, and back into a road, nearly wiping out a station wagon full of kids. Naturally I followed."

"To the bank?"

To several banks, as it turned out. Jack had cleaned out safety deposit boxes in two banks, money Broom conjectured was his profits from the drug operation. The lawyer stroked his tanned face with a powerful hand and spoke blandly of his discovery of the drugs in the door panel.

"That sounds like you knew where to look."

"Just luck."

The thought teased her nonetheless. This prominent prosperous lawyer, comfortable in his affluent setting, adoring wife, and admiring nephew in attendance, had gone to the truckstop, gotten into the van, and then unerringly located the hidden drugs.

"Why would you even look for something hidden?"

"A hunch."

But he laughed when he said it. Pascal thought that hunches would play little role in the professional thinking of Andrew Broom.

"Why did you want to see Jack? The mechanic."

"The woman my client Jerome Blatz is accused of killing lived next door to Jack Parry, in Bel Air, before his divorce. Afterward, she came looking for him at the truckstop."

"Looking for him?" Even as she asked the question, trying to get a chuckle into her voice, Pascal wanted to cry out in protest. Suddenly, added to her shame was a fear of what diseases such promiscuity made him vulnerable to, and if him, then her—and all the others, of course. But worse, far worse, was the implication of Andrew Broom's interest in Jack. He must think Jack had killed that woman.

"He's a pretty cool guy," Gerald said. "Stopping to pick up his money before he leaves town."

"If he even meant to leave town," Andrew said.

From her place he had gone to his former wife's where he had been picked up by bogus FBI agents. Pascal feared that his arrival at and departure from her apartment could not have gone unnoticed. Someone would remember and mention it and what would

191

Andrew Broom and Gerald Rowan and all the other people she had interviewed think of her then? She was a participant, not just a reporter, and as a reporter she was according herself special status. Her involvement with Jack Parry was privileged even while she was digging up everything she could about him and others. If it ever did become known that Jack Parry had shared her bed the night the search for him began, she would be discredited as a journalist, and not only in Wyler. A few years ago a woman lawyer fell in love with a client who was appealing his conviction and conspired with him to escape. Pascal wondered if she were any more professional.

When she was with Jack, her ambitions, her career, chatter about professionalism, had meant nothing. Theirs was a totally elemental relationship, a matter of gender, male and female, a silent impassioned possession of the other and then the exhausted falling apart into isolation. Had they ever had anything resembling a conversation?

Andrew Broom's confidence that Jack and not his client had killed Louise Long frightened Pascal. The lawyer was on the trail of one whose arrest would exonerate Jerome Blatz and he would leave no stone unturned until the arrest was made. Had Jack killed that woman? Pascal realized she didn't know if he were capable of such a thing. His behavior suggested contempt for women; he clearly saw them as disposable toys. His manner after a conquest was radically different from before and she could imagine his reaction if that former neighbor had made a nuisance of herself.

"So that's my statement," Andrew said, rising. "The innocence of my client was never in doubt, and the arrest of Jack Parry will put an end to a pretty cavalier use of prosecutorial power."

Pascal dutifully wrote it down. She did not yet leave

the office, as if being with Gerald negated the memories of Jack.

"You look beat."

"I feel great," she lied. "But suddenly Wyler is awash with news. Drugs, murder, Indians."

"Just when I thought the Indians were scalped, or skulled, the legislature decides to give back some land."

"It may be just beginning. The American Indian Movement called the paper and wanted to know just what tribe is involved."

"What's the answer?" he asked.

"I gave them Phillipa's number."

"The prospect of the return of real land might attract some real Indians. What proof is there that that's a burial ground? Apart from the one skull, that is?"

"Look, your uncle suggested the giveaway to Boyd Carlson."

"Andrew thinks he's an Indian."

"Really?"

"His people came from Cleveland."

That got her to her feet. In another mood, if he were free, she would find Gerald fun, but not now.

"I wonder if Phillipa ever really had the skull."

"I saw it."

"Who would steal it?"

"You got me."

He too was on his feet. "Where'd she get it?"

On the way through the reception area she gave him a quick account and it was only when she was going down in the elevator that it occurred to her that everything she had told him she had learned from Jack Parry.

THIRTY-EIGHT

Bonnie might have been relieved to hear of Jack's arrest if she could have overlooked the fact that he had fled to his former wife when danger threatened. What a dumb thing to do. Then he'd been hustled away from the house in Bel Air. That brought a mean little smile briefly to her lips, but she wiped it off, telling herself that he hadn't come to her because he wanted to spare her embarrassment. But none of that mattered now that she knew the FBI agents who had taken him away were phony.

"Oh oh," Phyllis said, looking goofier than usual.

"Oh oh, what?"

But she already knew Phyllis's theory that Jack was mixed up with the mob, forming the connection between Wyler and Chicago. If Phyllis was right, Jack was in far more danger now than he had ever been.

"If he's even alive," Phyllis whispered.

Bonnie could have hit her, but what if she was right? Jack was on the stuff, she knew that if no one else did,

194

and Phyllis wasn't the only one to jump to the conclusion that the drugs found in the door of that van had been meant for Jack. Bonnie just didn't want to think about it anymore and, when her shift ended, she stopped on the way home and splurged on a bottle of pretty good brandy. She meant to put on some tapes, get into bed and drink herself into sleep, something she hadn't done in a long time. The prospect was pleasant and she could almost feel the sweet numbing effect of the brandy when she turned into her driveway and saw the car parked there.

Jack? She was so excited, she scrambled from the car without the paper sack containing the brandy, and ran to the door. But the driver door of the parked car opened and Gerald Rowan stepped out.

"Could we talk?"

"No." She stomped back to her car and got the brandy.

"Just tell me where you got the skull."

"The skull!"

But he was serious. Bonnie began to laugh; she laughed while she unlocked the door and was still laughing when the lawyer followed her inside. She opened the cupboard and said over her shoulder, "You want a drink?"

"What are we having?"

She took two glasses into the living room and told him to pour while she powdered her nose. Powdered her nose. She said it without thinking. It was a phrase Jack used. He liked oddball, out of use phrases. "Going to make a phone call," was another way of going to the john. In the bathroom, she put her face close to the mirror. The tears in her eyes were from laughing. She wiped them dry and wished that she were alone so she could drink in peace.

"We've learned that you gave that skull to your brother," Gerald Rowan said, handing her a glass.

She tried her drink, liking the viscous feel of the brandy in her mouth, letting it slide down her throat leaving a thread of fire.

"No you haven't."

"Do you deny it?"

"Where would I have gotten a skull to give to anyone?"

"From Jack Parry."

She controlled her surprise. The only one who knew that was Phillipa and Bonnie could not imagine her telling Gerald Rowan or anyone else where she had gotten the skull, particularly now that it was missing. "We called it short sheeting in school," Gerald said, putting his glass on the coffee table. "What a shock it must have been to find that in your bed."

"Have you seen Jack?"

"Bonnie, every level of police in the state is looking for him."

"How did you know he put that thing in my bed?"

"I have to protect my sources," he said with feigned pomposity.

"You're no reporter . . ."

She stopped. Was that the explanation? She herself had told Phillipa but what if Jack had told that girl from the newspaper and she told Gerald. Bonnie felt doubly betrayed. It was bad enough that Jack slept with other women, but to tell that girl about a practical joke he'd played on her was far worse. Whenever she tried to get him to talk about his wife, he had given a look that made her shiver. Of course she hadn't asked him about anyone else, why would she, but he hadn't volunteered either. The sonofabitch. It was pretty clear where she stood in his life.

"What do you want to know?" she asked Gerald Rowan.

THIRTY-NINE

What made the skull that had passed from Jack Parry to Bonnie to Phillipa the same one the boy Tommy had found was the hole in the center of the forehead.

"Where the assassin's bullet entered," Phillipa said. She seemed to have vast reservoirs of righteous indignation. "I should have expected it would be stolen."

Andrew did not try to follow her thinking. There was the strong possibility that her husband, less caught up in her enthusiasms, had gotten rid of it. Clark Cooper seemed stunned by the success of his wife's efforts. The land the legislature had voted to return to its original owners presented difficulties, particularly since those with stronger claims to it were beginning to be heard from. Phillipa dismissed these rivals and apparently felt no need of legal advice on the matter, much to Andrew's relief. He was encouraging her plans for a ceremony at the burial grounds and would have been hard put to turn her down if she asked him to represent her claim to the land. Perhaps she couldn't bring herself to see other Native Americans as her enemy.

Jerome sat in the kitchen, behind the trestle table, his back pressed against the wall. Ever since his release, he had spent his days at home with Maud, finding her scented bright kitchen reassuring after his ordeal. Until the indictment was formally dropped, his feeling of vulnerability remained. Maybe it would never entirely go away. Maud poured Andrew a mug of coffee without asking if he wanted it and he sipped it standing. Jerome obviously wished Andrew had not come, finding the presence of his lawyer a reminder of things he was holed up in the kitchen to forget. But Andrew needed Jerome to feel guilty about the attempted disloyalty that had put him in harm's way.

"I want a look at the land you're giving away, Jerome."

"It was your idea!" Jerome glanced at Maud.

"Forty acres," Maud said dismissively. Andrew had the sense that she wouldn't mind getting Jerome out of her kitchen. "Forty acres you've got no use for."

It took Andrew fifteen minutes to persuade him. Jerome had to change shoes, then go to the bathroom, adjust his cap. "I think my head shrunk."

Maud made a noise.

They drove the pickup so that they could take a route through the farm and not go out on the county road. The springs in the truck were shot and the seat cushion was so flattened from use that they bounced painfully in the direction of the river. Jerome had both hands on the wheel, and his mouth was clamped shut as if he feared his denture would pop out. Andrew began to suspect that Jerome was making the ride as bumpy as he could. There was no point in talking until Jerome came to a stop at a fence.

"You wanna walk or stay with the truck?"

"Let's walk."

They got out and Jerome opened the gate to let them into the field. Jerome said he hadn't been out here since he took in the soybeans. He was scuffing along, head down, studying the field. Andrew was looking toward the stand of trees where the body of Louise Long had been found when suddenly the earth gave way beneath him and he fell, pitching forward into a narrow hole.

"Hey!" Jerome yelled. "Hey?"

Andrew's right hand sunk into soft damp dirt and his left elbow partially broke his fall. He pushed back and got one foot beneath him and regained his balance. He was hip deep in a hole which had been lightly covered with branches bound together with twine. The hole led down stepwise out of sight.

"What the hell is it?" Jerome asked.

"You got a flashlight in the truck, Jerome?"

"Sure do."

Andrew got out of the hole and Jerome went with an arm-swinging walk back toward the truck. He wasn't ten yards off before a face appeared from underground, looking up at Andrew. A boy's face. Tommy.

"You all right, mister?"

Andrew nodded. "What you got here, a cave?"

A nod. Jerome came back and stood beside Andrew. "What the hell you doing digging in my field, boy?"

"Can I come down and see?" Andrew asked.

"It's pretty dirty."

"I can't get much dirtier."

The boy shrugged and backed out of sight. Andrew stepped down and squeezed through a narrow entryway and came into a dugout four feet square. Tommy had lit a lantern flashlight and hung it from the ceiling.

"You dig this place all by yourself?"

"Yeah."

"This where you found the skull?"

Tommy went to a corner of the dugout and moved aside a crate. A headless skeleton lay in an odd posture, as if it had fallen or been thrown into the hole.

"An Indian?" Jerome asked. He had come grunting and straining through the entrance and now stood with Andrew, looking down at the dimly lit skeleton.

"Cover it up," Andrew said, and Tommy did.

The architecture of the dugout impressed Jerome and his manner changed as he asked Tommy how he had managed to get those beams in place and cover over the hole he had dug. Tommy had read about the building of the pyramids, he had read about getting those huge boulders to Stonehenge. Dragging logs fifty yards even by himself was child's play by comparison. Tommy's attitude toward being discovered had changed now that the two adults seemed impressed by what he had done.

"That the only Indian skeleton you dug up?" Jerome asked.

"That's no Indian," Tommy said.

Jerome looked at Andrew, then smiled at Tommy. "How can you tell?"

"By the shoes."

Perforated two-toned oxfords, brown and tan, showing signs of wear but otherwise in better condition than their erstwhile wearer.

"This ain't no moccasin, Andrew," Jerome said.

"There's a new grave too," Tommy said. "Want to see it?"

He let the two men leave the dugout first and then came up out of the earth to lead them across the field in the direction of the trees. He seemed to be heading for the place where Louise's body was found but he stopped before entering the stand of trees. It was a mound over which leaves and branches had been flung.

Perhaps they would have walked by without noticing it if Tommy had not pointed it out. But was it a grave?

"My spade's in the truck," Jerome said.

"I think we better let Earl Waffle handle this, Jerome."

Jerome made the call from his kitchen, with Maud looking on, the rhythm with which she kneaded dough altering as she listened.

Her husband was angry. "Now cut that out, Earl. That's not a damned bit funny. You just get your ass out here pronto."

"Jerome!" Maud cried.

He slammed down the phone, ignoring Maud. "The sonofabitch wanted to know if I'd done it again."

"I'll take Tommy home," Andrew said. "There's no need for him to be mixed up in this. No need to say anything to Earl about the dugout, at least for now, don't you agree?"

"I'll tell you what I'd like to say to Earl Waffle."

"Jerome!"

After dropping Tommy off at his mother's, Andrew headed back to the river again, parked by the public access, and then went on foot through the woods and on into the field. There was no sign of Earl or his deputies, no sign of the coroner. Where the hell were they? He could go back to his car and make a phone call. He looked toward Jerome's place and saw the approaching pickup. Behind it came two cruisers and then the coroner. It might have been a funeral procession, except that the body was already in the ground. Andrew had a good idea whose body it was.

He was right. Half an hour later, after trying unsuccessfully to get Jerome to do the digging, the deputies went to work until they were halted by Hank Skifton.

"Hold it, Rollie. That's a man's arm."

Rollie danced out of the hole and Hank took his place. Andrew was kneeling beside him when he carefully brushed away the dirt and exposed the dead face of Jack Parry. In the center of his forehead was a neat hole where the bullet had entered.

FORTY

The county road was closed, as teams of investigators—Earl Waffle and his deputies gratefully eclipsed by the state troopers and the IBI—swarmed over the staked-off land near the Tippecanoe River, supervising the exhuming of bodies. Crews had been brought in from local cemeteries for the grim business. The scene reminded Andrew Broom of the archaeological dig he had planned, but the culture that was being unearthed had little to do with Wyler and even less to do with the Indians who had lived here before the white man came.

"What is this?" Gerald said, lifting his gauze mask from his mouth to speak.

"A burying ground for gang victims is my guess."

That was borne out in subsequent days, when identifications began to be made, mainly through dental work. Meanwhile, several dental clinics in Chicago were burglarized and the pace of identifications slowed. Phillipa fell out of the news. It was doubtful that she could have gotten an interview if she ran naked down Tarkington

203

Avenue in mid-afternoon. Her fantasy about the significance of the skull found by Tommy Parry had been
proved groundless and generic pleas for justice for
Native Americans collided with American Indian
Movement's repudiation of Phillipa and Clark.

"And you were encouraging her to stage a burial rite,"
Susannah chided.

Andrew started to explain to her and Gerald that he'd
hoped that the ceremony would begin a project to
uncover and rebury any Indian remains discovered
there. The result, he was sure, would have been the
same one being reached now, thanks to Tommy's showing them the fresh grave. What irony that it should be
his father's.

"No wonder Jack Parry took off from the truckstop
when that drug drop got put off schedule."

"Because you came asking for him," Gerald said. "I
suppose that tells us all we have to know of his connection with the death of Louise Long."

"Gerald, that is quite a jump," Susannah said.

They were dining at the country club, seated near a
window from which the course was visible in the soft
twilight. Around them, the subdued sounds of clinking
silverware and china, murmuring conversations, an
occasional laugh, might have insulated them from the
grisly events that had played themselves out by the
Tippecanoe, but they could talk of nothing else.

"Why run if he had nothing to hide?" Gerald asked.

"Do you think Jack Parry killed that woman?"
Susannah asked Andrew.

It was a question Andrew was not ready to face. He
preferred to steer the conversation back to the locations
that had been turned up from time to time in Illinois,
burial grounds for the victims of gangland slayings, the
bodies as often as not those of former members.
Skimmers, trimmers, stoolies, a ruthless revenge enact-

ed and the body dumped in unconsecrated ground. A location was used for a time, then abandoned for another. The identified bodies exhumed from beside the Tippecanoe were of persons missing at most six years before. The disappearance of gang members understandably did not engage the full attention of the police forces. Perhaps there were some who were grateful to the gang for doing the state's business.

Jack Parry had met the same fate as the others whose bodies were buried near the river. Frank McGough's clients had purchased some of the land where bodies were found, but not all. Andrew was certain a connection between the bodies and the urgency with which McGough's clients bought up the land could be established. But the likelihood of that happening had diminished when Bink Philips and Wendell Jensen came into the office and announced that the deals for purchasing their land had been called off.

"Why?"

Bink's eyes narrowed. "Who'd want to buy land full of bodies?"

"So what are you going to do?"

"How much did the state give Jerome for his parcel?"

"Nothing."

"C'mon. Look, Andrew, we weren't as upfront with you as we should have been, but . . ."

"You broke an agreement with Jerome Blatz that you all made here in this office. An agreement with one another and an agreement with me."

Wendell nodded. "You're right. If you just threw us out of here, no one would blame you."

"What we've been thinking is this," Bink said. "Throw our land in with Jerome's and that would make a far more impressive area for a commemorative park."

"For those bodies?"

"For the Indians!"

"You want to give your land to the Indians?"

Bink got control of himself and managed a pained smile. "I'll give my land on the same basis Jerome gave his."

"That's very generous of you."

"How much did they give Jerome, Andrew?"

"You're too late, gentlemen."

The legislature's reaction to the exhuming of the victims of gangland killings was to request and get a gubernatorial veto of the bill that had deeded the land over to the Native Americans represented by Clark and Phillipa Cooper. The objections of the American Indian Movement was a further spur. If the prospective buyers of Bink's and Wendell's land had reneged so had the state of Indiana.

"We are in the *status quo ante*," Andrew said, rising to signal that the appointment was ended.

"We can't farm that land now, Andrew. I wouldn't graze cows on it."

"Give it to the city for a park."

In the country club dining room Gerald said, "Do you think Jack Parry killed Louise?"

Andrew let the question pass a second time. He did not think Jack had killed Louise and his doubts were strengthened by Bonnie. The waitress was not at the Indy Truckstop, having taken extended sick leave since he had last spoken to her.

"I can't stand even to see Phyllis after what's happened," she had said. "You ever know someone who won't say I told you so but that's all they're saying anyway? Body language, whatever." Bonnie shook her head. Her great romance had ended in tragedy and she wanted to mourn alone. Her words bore the unmistakable scent of brandy.

"Everyone says he was the best mechanic in the world."

"He was a good man! He had his weakness, but it

was a man's weakness, something you have to expect. Show me a man who doesn't cat around and I'll show you an ugly sonofabitch."

She came out onto her patio and sank into a chair. Andrew sat beside her.

"Do you think he killed Louise?"

She turned and looked at him sadly. "Why would he?"

"Because she was pestering him?"

"In what way?"

"Do you think they were lovers?"

"I don't know. Maybe. If she was willing, Jack would have been."

This made more sense than the idea of Jack Parry repudiating a willing woman, bashing her head with a shovel because she was after his body. For Jack, as for Don Giovanni, anything in a skirt would do—or out of one.

"Yes," Andrew said in the country club in answer to Gerald's question and then at last they got onto something else.

Jerome of course was relieved. "When those tests on my shovel came back, I thought I was a goner, Andrew."

"They still had to prove it was your shovel," Andrew said, thankful he had not had to grasp at such straws.

"With my initials on it?"

"What do you mean?"

"All my tools have my initials on them. I'll show you."

Jerome took him out to a lean-to next to the barn that served as toolroom and workshop. Any tool with a wooden handle had JB burned into it. "This was a woodburning set my son Jeff had when he was a kid." The metal tools had JB scratched into their surface. Andrew nodded.

"You might have said this was why you knew that shovel wasn't yours."

"I said someone must have used my shovel."

RALPH McINERNY

"I thought it wasn't his shovel," Earl said with a know-ing grin when Andrew asked to see the murder weapon.

"It isn't. I haven't come to take it. I just want to see."

"Well, I wouldn't give it to you. It's still the murder weapon. We find who killed her, this will still be impor-tant."

There was no JB burned into the handle of the shov-el. "Thanks, Earl."

"That all?"

"You've seen one shovel, you've seen them all."

"Not all of them killed a woman, Andrew."

Andrew imagined himself developing an argument based on the absence of initials before a jury. But more than one juror would think, maybe Jerome hadn't got-ten around to branding this tool yet. The murder weapon was not old but it was not new either. Earl apparently accepted the *Dealer* view that Jack Parry had murdered Louise Long. So had the prosecutor. Andrew's client had been released. Was he the only one in town who saw Jerome's exoneration as pure luck?

The thought he did not want to think came to him first in sleep, his unconscious forcing it on him, and in the morning he remembered and felt his heart sink. If the incriminating shovel found in Jerome's truck did not belong to Jerome, it had been put there by the one who killed Louise, by someone with a shovel he could substitute for Jerome's. Tommy's dugout and the work it represented put the kid in the area and with a shovel. Had Louise become more than a nosy pest in the boy's mind, someone he would swing a shovel at, kill? It was difficult to read the mind of the son of Jack Parry.

"You take a shovel out there when you made the dugout, Tommy?"

A nod.

"From home?"

208

"Yes."

"Where is it?"

"I took it back."

"Took it back?"

"I borrowed it."

"When was that?"

"After I finished the cave."

"How long ago would that have been?"

He shrugged. "Couple weeks, I guess. Maybe more."

Andrew could have hugged the kid. He smiled at Ellen Parry like a fool.

"Who did you borrow it from?"

"Next door."

"Is it there now?"

"I suppose."

"Show me."

After he returned from the Long garage, Andrew sat down with Tommy and his mother and told them what they were about to do.

"It's not the Christian thing to say, Mr. Broom, but I'm glad the bastard is dead." Willis Long in shirtsleeves had been frowning at a computer screen when Andrew entered his office.

"Because of your wife?"

Willis pulled at his dewlaps with his meaty hand, nodded.

Andrew said, "If Jack Parry killed her."

"Isn't that why they let Jerome Blatz off?"

"Well, they can't indict a dead man. I guess it will just have to remain conjecture."

"It's no conjecture at all. He killed her. He was there. That's public knowledge."

Pascal's story in the *Dealer* developed the premise that Jack Parry had killed his estranged lover and in an unrelated matter run afoul of his gang connections.

"Everything would have turned on the shovel," Andrew said. "In a trial, I mean."

"They ran tests on it, didn't they?"

"Oh, it's the murder weapon all right. No doubt about that."

"So what's the problem?"

"The shovel isn't Jerome's. If he had ever been brought to trial, that would have been sufficient to get him acquitted."

Willis shook his head. "It's too complicated for me. I'm just glad it's all over."

"Amen."

Andrew stood and went to the door, stopping on the way to examine one of the garish pictures that hung on the wall of Willis Long's office. "If we knew whose shovel was used to kill your wife . . ." He stopped. "Where did you get this picture?"

"I don't know."

"Nice."

"I like it."

"Jerome's shovel had his initials burned into the handle. I suppose the killer switched his for Jerome's. He must have taken it with him. You ever want to get rid of this picture, let me know."

Outside, Andrew waited in his car down the street from the building that housed Willis Long's office. Five minutes later, Willis came through the revolving doors onto the sidewalk and hurried up the street. Andrew waited until Willis turned into the parking lot at the corner. Monthly rates. Willis's blue Olds was parked there. Andrew had his car in gear and, when the Olds appeared, followed. Andrew punched out the number on his phone.

"Yes?"

"Mrs. Parry? He's on his way. Is Tommy all set?"

"Yes."

All the eloquence of a mother's anxiety was contained in the two syllables she had spoken. But she understood the importance of what they were doing, Tommy, Ellen, and himself. He did not want to get too close to Willis. Staying behind had its risks, however, and sure enough just as the Olds went through an intersection half a block ahead of Andrew the light turned yellow. He floored the gas pedal, but when he went through the intersection the light had already turned red. An angry horn commented on what he had done. Approaching in the opposite lane was a cruiser. Andrew stared straight ahead, wearing a look of concerned innocence. The cruiser pulled over, its turn signal flashing, about to execute a U-turn. Damn it. At the corner, he took a right and immediately turned into an alley, doubling back. He did not want to be caught between a pursuing cop and the blue Olds.

He came back onto Tarkington and once more headed toward Bel Air. Willis was no longer in sight. And then, in his rearview mirror, the cruiser came into view. Andrew stomped on the gas. It took him ten minutes to shake the cruiser, his escape including a nerve-wracking stretch against traffic on a one-way street, but finally he was sure he was alone and he sped to Bel Air.

He parked in front of the Parry house. The blue Olds was in the driveway next door. Andrew ran across the lawn to the front door, which was held open by Ellen Parry. He went through the house to the back door just in time to see Willis Long emerge from his garage. He was carrying a shovel. He held it against his body and walked stiffly to the Olds. He unlocked the trunk and just as the door yawned open the police cruiser nosed into the curb in front of Andrew's car. Andrew came outside and started toward the Olds. Willis Long looked at Andrew and then at the deputy who had gotten out of the cruiser, uniformed, belted, armed, the personification of retributive justice. A wild expression came into Willis's eye, and he gripped the handle of the shovel, and took a batter's stance. The deputy came across the lawn, his hand resting on his pistol.

"Who owns that car?"

Ellen Parry and Tommy appeared and Andrew was about to shout at them to go back inside when Willis seemed to shrink into himself. He flung the shovel from him and sank to his knees, covered his face with his hands, and began to sob. Andrew picked up the shovel with JB burned into its handle.

"Deputy, take him downtown and book him."

"He the speeder?"

"No. He murdered his wife."

FORTY-ONE

The prosecutor's problem was persuading Willis Long to plead innocent. He refused. "I killed her. I want to pay for it. Why waste time and the taxpayer's money? Put me away."

"It's not that simple, Willis. There has to be a trial."

"There's nothing to try. I killed her. I would have stood by and let Jerome Blatz take the blame. I would have let people think Jack Parry did it. Prison is too good for me."

"You ever see a prison, Willis?"

Willis looked around. He had been in jail a week. The prosecutor tried to tell him that the county jail was a resort compared to where he was liable to end up.

"Plead insanity."

"I'm as sane as you."

"Then plead insanity. You'd be crazy not to."

Eventually he did plead insanity. Boyd Carlson suggested that his letters to the *Dealer* could be put in evidence. He had announced he would not run for reelection after he had assured the defeat of his own bingo bill but the only one who seemed to care was his wife. Clark Cooper had gone on an epic drunk and was being nursed back to health by a Phillipa now content to supervise bingo at the Bison and forget about transposing historic grievances into a personal key. "We are all murderers," roared Grover Layton from his pulpit. "We are thieves and traitors, name it, no sin is too vile for any of us to commit." He seemed almost jealous of Willis Long. Gerald squeezed Julie's hand. "I think I'm getting religion." "Or vice versa." "What's the difference?" "Between versa and vice?" Gerald could hardly wait for the congregation to leap to its feet so he could take her in his arms.

"Andrew," Susannah asked, "why would he have taken Jerome's shovel home and put it in his garage?"

"He's pleading insanity."

"But what if he had just gotten rid of it?"

What if he hadn't broken down and confessed? What if his remorse had not overcome him? What if Andrew hadn't run a stoplight and inadvertently brought a sheriff cruiser to the scene at the appropriate moment?

"What if you and I go upstairs and read in bed?"

"Read?"

"Braille."

Ralph McInerny, author of numerous novels, including the Father Dowling mysteries and a series written under the pseudonym Monica Quill, is the Michael P. Grace Professor of Medieval Studies at the University of Notre Dame.